stardust stables

SUNSET IN THE WEST

stardust stables

SUNSET IN THE WEST

SABLE HAMILTON

stripes

STRIPES PUBLISHING
An imprint of Little Tiger Press
1 The Coda Centre, 189 Munster Road,
London SW6 6AW

A paperback original
First published in Great Britain in 2014

Text copyright © Jenny Oldfield, 2014
Photographic images courtesy of
www.gettyimages.co.uk © Anna Gorin
and www.shutterstock.com

ISBN: 978-1-84715-443-9

For Shelley, my fearless friend

chapter one

"Filming in Alaska – rather you than me!" Hayley told Becca. "It'll be so-o-o-o cold!"

"But I get to work with an amazing director and a whole bunch of 'A' list actors," Becca insisted as she stowed Pepper's saddle in the Stardust Stables trailer. "What's not to like?"

"Yeah, but it's not here in beautiful, big-sky Colorado – it's in the f-f-frozen n-n-north!" Hayley replied. "Brrr!"

"Who cares? At least it's a job."

"Ouch!" Hurt by Becca's words, Hayley stepped back to let Becca lead her grey Quarter Horse into the back of the trailer. She felt bad because it was the end of the summer and so far she hadn't landed a contract for her junior stunt-riding stables – unlike Becca who had done two weeks' work on the long-running

Gold Rush TV series and was now headed up north for a stunt-double role in *Wolfman 2.*

"Sorry," Becca murmured. "I didn't mean..."

"No, you're right. I need to get my act together."

It wasn't only Becca's success that worried Hayley. Take Kami – the newbie at Stardust Stables. Practically the moment she'd got here, she and her horse Magic had worked on *Moonlight Dream* with Coreen Kessler. Then Alisa and Diabolo's stunt work had featured in *Wildfire* and more recently Kellie and Dylan had worked on a low-budget independent movie, based in Hayley's home town of Jackson Hole. Everyone was doing great things except her.

Becca loaded Pepper in then closed up the trailer. "Something will come along soon," she told Hayley. "I'll be freezing my butt off in Alaska with Callie Hooper for three whole days and suddenly it'll happen for you, just you wait."

Ouch again! Callie Hooper was the fourteen-year-old rider from Pete Mason's rival High Noon Stables who'd gone up against Hayley for the second *Wolfman 2* role. It had been a close-run thing but in the end the casting director had chosen Callie over Hayley.

"Oops!" Becca realized she'd said the wrong thing again.

"No, really." Hayley took it on the chin. "I'm happy for you and Pepper. I was kidding about the frozen north. You know me."

"Yeah, always the joker." Becca was in a hurry to find Jack, the co-owner of Stardust Stables, and let him know they were ready to leave for the airport. "So I'll see you later in the week," she told Hayley. "Unless you land that big job you're always dreaming of, in which case you'll be away filming who knows where."

"Yeah, unless that happens." Hayley put on a brave smile. "Anyway, I'd better go too – I'm supposed to be working with Cool Kid in the round pen. Lizzie will kill me if I'm late. Bye!"

And she ran from the sunny yard into the tack room to fetch her horse's saddle.

"You won't need that saddle or the bridle today," Lizzie told Hayley when she found her fifteen minutes later, tacking up in the corral. "In fact, no one will."

Zak and Tom were bringing in horses from the

meadow and lining them up in the corral ready for a day's work with their riders.

"How come?" Hayley asked, taking off Cool Kid's saddle and balancing it on the rail.

Lizzie patted Cool Kid's neck then rubbed his long, flat nose with her knuckles. "Because today I thought we'd try a little bareback riding for a change."

"Cool!" Hayley liked the sound of that. It would be new and exciting and it would help her to stay focussed on something positive instead of brooding over her failure to get the *Wolfman 2* job.

Running the flat of her hand down Cool Kid's neck and along his broad brown and white back, Lizzie told her that she thought the little Paint horse would do well. "He has low withers and a pretty smooth gait – all good for riding without a saddle. Compare him with Diabolo, for instance."

Hayley stood back to get a good view of Alisa's long-limbed, elegant sorrel mare who stood tethered and patiently waiting for her rider to show up.

"Too high in the withers," Lizzie pointed out. "Which means she automatically throws her rider's balance back from the vertical. You have to compensate for that and pay attention."

"I get it," Hayley nodded and started to size up the other horses. "Dylan should be good though. Magic not so much. When do we start?"

The trainer looked at her watch. "As soon as the others show up. Do you know where they are?"

"Tom and Zak are out in the meadow and I guess the rest are still having breakfast."

Before Lizzie could add anything, Hayley had sprinted out of the corral towards the ranch house. "Come on, y'all," she yelled from the entrance to the large dining room. "Ross, Alisa, Kami, Kellie, everyone – Lizzie's out there waiting. We're about to go bareback riding!"

The seven young riders sat astride their horses without saddles or bridles, taking in Lizzie's instructions.

"As always when you ride, focus on where you want to go. Look ahead, not down." Their trainer took them back to basics, standing in the centre of the round pen, hands on hips, with her fair hair hidden under a broad-brimmed black Stetson. "Keep your legs forward, with heels down and toes up – the same position as if you're riding with stirrups."

"Tell me something I don't already know," Ross grumbled under his breath. His horse, Jack D, a light sorrel with a white flash down his nose, shifted impatiently under him. "This stuff is plain common sense to anyone who's been around horses all their lives."

"Jeez, Ross, just because you grew up in rodeo-land," Tom sniped back. "Doesn't mean bareback riding comes easy to the rest of us."

"We're going to move in a line clockwise round the pen," Lizzie instructed. "Begin with walk then into trot. Once you're all happy with that, I'll ask you to lope."

"You hear that?" Hayley leaned forward to whisper into Cool Kid's ear. "You're not wearing a bit or a bridle, so you have to listen extra hard to what I'm asking you to do with my shifts of balance and pressure from my legs."

Cool Kid pricked up his little fox ears and tossed his dark mane. Freshly brushed by Hayley, the nut-brown patches on his coat were the colour of shiny sweet chestnuts while the white areas shone like pure fresh snow.

"Good boy," Hayley murmured. She checked that

her lead rope was clipped safely to either side of his head collar, forming a loop that she would use as a substitute for his usual split reins.

"And remember," Lizzie told them, "if you lose balance at a lope, don't be embarrassed to grab your horse's mane, but don't grip with your thighs or pull on his head."

"Grip mane," Hayley repeated slowly to herself, while Kami glanced nervously at Alisa. Even gutsy, daredevil Kellie looked unsure.

"OK, team, are we ready?" Lizzie called at last.

"Ready!" they chorused.

"So, Hayley, I want you to lead the group. Walk Cool Kid out nice and easy so the others can follow."

Eagerly Hayley followed the instruction but she had to admit that it felt weird to ride bareback – something she hadn't done since she was a little kid at home in Jackson Hole.

She'd snuck out of town on her bike early one morning and on to the neighbou___ property. There she'd stolen a sec___ their cow horses – a big dark bay ___ he felt her sitting securely on his b___ a flat run across their meadow, tossing her up in the air, forcing her to cling on to his mane for dear life until he'd screeched to a halt two strides short of a four-foot fence. She'd breathed a sigh of relief and slid to the ground, knees wobbling. Luckily no one had seen her wild ride and she'd never mentioned it to a single soul. Still, it ranked in her memory as one of the highlights of her childhood in Wyoming.

"This is so weird!" Tom complained, letting his Palomino horse, Legend, bunch up too close behind Hayley.

"Sit forward on to his withers," Lizzie told him. "Heels down. Now trot."

Behind Tom and Legend, Alisa was struggling to keep her balance on Diabolo. In spite of what Lizzie had told them earlier, she was tempted to grip her horse's sides with her thighs. "Deep breath," she told herself. "Good girl, Diabolo, nice and easy."

Diabolo listened and fell into a smoother rhythm, ahead of Kami and Magic then Zak and his high-maintenance Appaloosa, Ziggy.

"This sucks!" Zak complained as Ziggy threw him up ᵉ air with every short, choppy step. He was glad when Lizzie called for Hayley to break into a lope and he could sit back and let his body relax.

"But it's fun!" Kellie cried. Dylan was built for bareback riding, she decided. His ears were flicked forward and he was loving every second.

"Whoa!" Behind Kellie and Dylan, Ross and Jack D brought up the rear. As his sorrel lunged forward and almost took a bite out of Dylan's broad butt, Ross grabbed a fistful of mane to try and stay on but failed miserably, toppling sideways and landing like a sack of potatoes in the dirt.

Watching from the centre of the round pen, Hayley grinned. "Oops! Hey, Ross, I thought you said bareback riding was plain common sense!"

Ross stood up and brushed himself down. "Freak accident," he muttered. "Jack D spooked at nothing. Won't happen again."

"Says you." Hayley enjoyed the sight of Jack D waiting patiently while Ross re-mounted, and she noticed that Ross was kind of cute when he got embarrassed.

"OK, I take back what I said earlier," Ross mumbled as he rode into the pen. "Bareback riding takes a lot more practice than I thought."

★ ★ ★ ★ ★

"The good thing about this style of riding is that you get more physical contact so it creates an extra special bond between you and your horse."

"Yeah, I already feel that." Eager to learn more, Hayley had stayed behind in the round pen with Lizzie long after the others had gone in for lunch.

"The bad thing is there's a higher risk of injury," continued Lizzie.

"How come?"

"It's obvious when you think about it." Lizzie watched Hayley get ready to run ten metres then leap on to Cool Kid. "If your horse spooks when you're riding in a saddle, you have the saddle horn to grab hold of. Plus your balance is more secure with your feet in stirrups. Plus again - you have much more control over your horse when he has a metal bit in his mouth."

"Got it." Hayley took heed of the warning. "So shall we go again?"

"You betcha!"

Hayley set her mind on the task then sprinted to where Cool Kid stood in the centre of the pen. She took a giant sideways, split-legged leap, judging it perfectly and landing dead in the centre of his broad back. Her sturdy horse stood still as a statue, without flinching. "So tell me – if it's so dangerous, why are we doing it?" she asked her trainer.

"Because!" Lizzie said with an enigmatic shrug. She pulled her phone out of her pocket and clicked on camera mode. "OK, now this time go straight from walk into lope – no trot."

"You're going to video this?" Hayley asked, squeezing lightly with her legs. Cool Kid stepped out briskly in the empty arena.

"Yes, but ignore me," Lizzie replied. "Have fun. Lope on until I tell you to stop."

"You heard what Lizzie said – we're a 'natural bareback team'!" It was early evening and Hayley rode Cool Kid out into the meadow after a hard day's work in the round pen. She felt the skin of her face and neck prickle after hours in the hot sun. Her back ached and her legs were tired but she was happy when she remembered Lizzie's parting comment.

Cool Kid knew that his rider was pleased. He picked up his feet smartly and turned his head from time to time to give the toe of her boot a friendly nibble.

"Quit that!" she laughed, knowing full well that he would take no notice. She rode him out along the dirt track past the red barn towards the meadow where the other horses were already eating hay from the circular feeding rack. "What do you say we chill for a while?" she asked, riding on past the gate towards the creek. "You can take a drink, we can look at the sunset together."

They ambled on along the track and through some willows until they came to the water's edge.

"Did you see Lizzie shooting that video?" Hayley asked Cool Kid as he lowered his head and slurped from the clear creek. "Wasn't it weird how she wouldn't tell me why she was filming us?"

He took long, eager gulps, taking no notice of Hayley as she slid to the ground then leaned lazily against him.

It was deliciously cool in the shade of the rustling willows, with the sun sinking behind Clearwater Peak, turning the mountains black and spreading a fiery red glow along the horizon.

"You know what I reckon," Hayley went on, folding

her arms and resting her head against Cool Kid's shoulder. "I'm guessing she filmed it to show to someone she knows in the movie industry – a director, maybe. She wouldn't tell me what it was for because she didn't want to raise my hopes. Plus, she wanted us to be totally relaxed."

Cool Kid stopped drinking and raised his head to turn and nibble at the hem of her dusty white T-shirt.

"Stop it!" she laughed, gently turning his head away. "And OK, you're right, maybe I am reading too much into the video situation and it wasn't a secret audition after all."

Cool Kid sighed and gazed up at the setting sun.

"You know me though – always looking on the bright side."

He sighed again.

"Hey," she said, unhooking one end of his lead rope to walk him back to the meadow. "You're right – I shouldn't get my hopes up!"

They walked on in silence for a while then Hayley stopped to look straight into Cool Kid's dark brown eyes. "But really, this could be it. This could be the big deal we've been waiting for all summer!"

chapter two

"You and Cool Kid were far and away the best performers in the round pen today," Kellie told Hayley over supper that evening.

"You did pretty good, too," Hayley replied through a mouthful of baked potato. She'd loosened her dark hair from the tight braids she wore when she worked and her kinked locks fell over her shoulders. She hadn't had time to shower and still had on the frayed T-shirt, jeans and dusty boots she'd been wearing all day.

"It's partly down to our horses, I guess." Kellie had moved on from her main course to a dessert of home-made apple pie and ice cream. "Like Lizzie said, it helps that Dylan and Cool Kid have low withers and a smooth gait."

"But mostly it's down to the way you two ride," Kami

insisted from across the table. "Your butts stick to your horses' backs like they're superglued in place!"

"Thanks ... I think!" Hayley giggled. "All I know is that I ache in parts of my body that I didn't even know existed!"

"Yeah, my poor shoulders have stiffened up." Alisa groaned as she reached for a second helping of pie. "I found it hard to relax out there today. And did you hear Lizzie threaten us with more bareback practice tomorrow?"

"Yeah, what's she up to?" Kellie wondered.

"She said to only show up if you want to," Ross reminded them. "No one's going to force you."

"Which means Hayley will do it," Kellie grinned. "I've never known her to wimp out on a challenge, not ever."

"You're right," Hayley agreed. "Aching all over or not, I'll be there at 8 a.m. sharp!"

"Ross and Jack D, Kellie and Dylan and Hayley and Cool Kid." Standing in the gateway to the round pen, Lizzie checked names off her list. "Who else is volunteering for a second bout of torture?"

"Not Kami and Alisa," Ross replied. "They took a ride into town to buy new hat bands and stampede strings. Plus Kami's mom is driving in from Elk Creek especially to catch up." After yesterday's bruising experience he'd been tempted to join Kami and Alisa, until Hayley had challenged him at breakfast.

"Girls make better bareback riders than boys," she'd claimed, staring him right in the eye. "We have a lower centre of gravity, that's why."

"No way!" He'd almost choked on his crispy bacon.

"So come out again today and prove it." Hayley had thrown down the gauntlet and he couldn't refuse.

"And Tom – does anyone know where he is?" Lizzie asked now.

"He stayed with Zak in the corral to help the farrier shoe five of our horses," Kellie explained.

"Cool." Lizzie seemed satisfied that only the riders who really wanted to continue were present. "So, the same as yesterday – head up, straight back, heels down, toes up..."

"...Sore butts, stiff shoulders..." Hayley continued under her breath. "...Blisters, bruises, sun damage and exhaustion!"

"This is natural horsemanship, the way the natives rode soon after the Spanish first introduced horses into North America." Lizzie described how men from the Mohican, Apache and Arapaho tribes had rounded up wild horses and put them to use as a means of transport. "The young braves must have looked spectacular when they rode bareback into battle, carrying spears decorated with beads and feathers, with bows and arrows strapped to their backs."

Lizzie's description sent a shiver of excitement through Hayley.

Ross leaned over to mutter in her ear. "How about that? You heard what she said – 'young braves'... as in, guys!"

"So?" Hayley knew what was coming next but she refused to play along.

"Wasn't it you who swore that girls made better bareback riders than guys?"

"Just watch and learn, OK?" she said with a grin as Lizzie gave them their first task.

"One clockwise circuit around the pen at a lope," the trainer told them. "Then neck-rein with the lead rope and use your left leg to steer your horse away from the fence towards the centre. You see the jump I've built there? I want you and your horse to clear it and run straight out through the open gate into the corral. Wait there for the others to finish. Hayley, you and Cool Kid take a first shot at it."

Lizzie was filming again, Hayley noticed. But she had no time to let the camera make her nervous as she launched Cool Kid from walk straight into lope. She settled easily into the rocking rhythm then turned him towards the jump. He took off and landed smooth as anything then loped out through the gate. She grinned and patted Cool Kid's sweating neck. Superglue Girl and her Paint horse had delivered!

"OK, now Ross!" Lizzie kept on filming.

"Remember I'm the only guy here," Ross whispered to Jack D. "We've got plenty to prove, you and me."

With a cheeky grin at Hayley he pushed his light sorrel gelding into a lope, holding the looped lead rope in his one hand and sweeping his hat from his head with the other to wave it high in the air. He was still waving it and whooping with pleasure as Jack D cleared the jump.

"Good job," Kellie said from outside the pen.

"Don't tell him that," Hayley joked. "His head's already too big for his hat!"

Kellie was next and she was determined not to let the others outshine her. "Let's go!" she told Dylan, who got round the circuit at a flat run, swung in towards the jump and leaped cleanly over it. "Yee-hah!" Kellie cried as she and Dylan shot out through the gate.

"OK, everyone, a little less of the rodeo action, please," Lizzie called. "Come back into the round pen. We'll slow down the pace a little, try side-stepping and backing off like we do in a dressage arena. If it all goes smoothly, we'll break for lunch then move on to some of the really tricky stuff this afternoon."

"Another one down, two to go," Ross said when he and Jack D plus Hayley and Cool Kid assembled in the round pen after lunch.

"What happened to Kellie?" Lizzie asked when she joined them.

"Dylan threw a shoe." Ross wanted Lizzie to know that one of their star riders hadn't wimped out. "Kellie needed to catch the farrier before he left."

Lizzie nodded and continued briskly. "OK, Hayley, so we'll start with the running, sideways mount that you and Cool Kid perfected yesterday. Ross, watch closely."

Eagerly Hayley positioned her horse, told him to stay in place then took ten paces back. She sprinted and leaped clean on to his back, where she took up the looped lead rope and trotted him on around the pen.

"Ross, it's your turn," Lizzie called.

He copied Hayley's routine but when he came to leap astride Jack D, his horse took a nervy sideways step and Ross landed in the dirt. "Ouch," he grumbled as he picked himself up.

Hayley smiled. Why was her heartbeat speeding up whenever Ross was around these days? And why did his sheepish grin send her light-headed and giddy?

"Again!" Lizzie called. "We work at this until it's one hundred per cent perfect. Let's go!"

That afternoon, Hayley and Ross learned to use the speed of their approach to place both hands flat on their horses' withers, raise their weight off their mount and spin on their hands like gymnasts on a pommel.

"Move on!" Lizzie called as soon as she was satisfied.

Next they learned to mount bareback and stand up, arms outspread as their horses walked, trotted then loped on.

"What's up? Are we going to work at a circus, or what?" Ross muttered to Hayley.

"Search me, but something's in the air because Lizzie is still videoing the whole thing," she replied.

From standing they went to sitting again and learning to make their horses rear up without the help of bridle, saddle or stirrups.

"Ouch!" said Ross. Jack D had reared and Ross had lost hold of the improvised reins. He'd slid back, clean over his horse's rump and experienced his third bumpy landing.

When it was her turn, Hayley threw her balance forward as Cool Kid reared and pawed the air. He pranced on his hind legs and she stayed put without grabbing the mane.

"Yee-hah!" Ross yelled encouragement, impressed by the rodeo-style stunt.

"I give in," he told Hayley at the end of the session. "Superglue Girl takes the bareback prize, no contest!"

"She totally does," Lizzie confirmed. "Ross, you can take your horse into the corral and give him some loving. But Hayley, I want you and Cool Kid to try one more thing, out by the creek. Do you have enough gas left in the tank?"

"Sure," Hayley agreed, eager as ever.

It took them ten minutes to walk out to the bend in Elk Creek that Lizzie had chosen. It was beyond the willows, out of sight of the ranch, where the water in the creek ran smooth and deep.

"Wait for me to climb up on to this rock," Lizzie instructed. "Once I'm in position, I want you to lope Cool Kid through the creek."

"Through?" Hayley repeated. Not across to the opposite bank, but following the course of the stream.

Lizzie nodded then scrambled up the dome-shaped rock. "As far as the next stand of pine trees, then stop. Got it?"

Hayley judged the distance. It was about a hundred metres. They would be riding into the low sun, which would make things more difficult. But she trusted Cool Kid to keep his footing on the rocky, uneven bed of the stream. "No tricks, no stunts?" she checked.

"Just plain old loping," Lizzie said, raising her camera and training it on horse and rider. "OK, ready - go!"

Hayley walked Cool Kid into the water, which was half a metre deep at the starting point, but which she knew could go deeper or shallower without warning. She pointed him towards the pine trees, pressed her legs against his sides, sat back and clicked her tongue.

Whoosh! Cool Kid took off. He plunged through the water, sending up ice-cold spray that showered down on to Hayley's bare face and arms. Within seconds she was soaked from head to foot.

Cool Kid ploughed on, his hooves knocking against loose rocks and displacing them, plunging his rider forwards and sideways in an erratic lope towards the trees. Sunlight caught the cold spray, which glittered like a million diamonds. As they sped on, Hayley partly closed her eyes against the glare, trusting Cool Kid to stay upright and to keep her safe.

"So cool!" she said to herself. Sunlight and spray, a spectacular lope through water and all captured on camera. "I honestly believe I've died and gone to heaven!"

chapter three

Early next morning, Tom knocked on the girls' bunkhouse door.

"It's OK, I'll get it – I'm already dressed," Kami told Alisa, who was just out of the shower. She also beat Kellie and Hayley to the door. "Hi, Tom," she said.

The other girls saw her blush then smile.

"Aw, sweet!" Hayley whispered when she saw the two of them together. She was about to return to the room she shared with Kellie when Tom called her back.

"Actually, Hayley, it's you I need to talk to."

"Me? Why, what did I do?"

"Well, apparently, you loped your horse bareback through the creek," he replied, still with eyes only for Kami. "That's what Lizzie said."

"Hey, there's nothing wrong with Cool Kid, is there?"

Hayley's heart skipped a beat. "He didn't get hurt, did he?"

"No, relax. This is about Cool Kid, but not in a bad way."

"Oh, Tom, just spit it out," Kellie told her brother. "Can't you see you're tying Hayley in knots?"

At last Tom tore his gaze away from Kami and focused on his errand. "OK, so Lizzie told me to tell you that she sent the video of you and Cool Kid to her director buddy in England and the footage went down well. Apparently she's auditioning stunt riders for a new movie and Lizzie's hoping this could lead to something big."

"England?" Hayley echoed, stepping out on to the porch and looking down towards the meadow. She was relieved to spot her horse frisking by the hay feeder with Diabolo and Dylan. "That's a million miles away."

"Yeah, it would cost a fortune to get Hayley and Cool Kid over there to audition," Kellie pointed out.

"It turns out that's why Lizzie has been filming Hayley in the round pen – as a kind of long-distance audition," Tom explained. "And it's the reason why she wants you to be in her tack-room office in – let's see – five minutes from now."

"Why the big rush? Jeez, I'm not even dressed..." Hayley panicked, gazing down at her bare feet and tugging her loose hair back into the stretchy band that she slipped from her wrist.

"Five minutes," Tom repeated before saying a reluctant bye to Kami then heading down to the barn to carry on loading fresh hay on to the trailer.

"I still don't get it," Hayley gasped, checking her watch before running back to her room and sticking her feet into the nearest pair of boots, which happened to be Kellie's old ones and two sizes too big. She threw on a denim jacket over her T-shirt then took a quick look in the mirror. "My hair!" she wailed, clutching at stray locks and pushing them behind her ears.

"It doesn't matter – go!" Kellie and Alisa told her as she emerged from her room. They shunted her down the corridor and out of the door. "Run, Hayley – you've only got two minutes," they yelled after her.

Hayley sprinted from the bunkhouse, down the hill, across the corral and into the tack room. She was out of breath as she knocked on Lizzie's office door.

"Come in!" Lizzie called, her back to the door and studying her computer screen when Hayley entered. "How do you feel about auditioning on Skype?" she asked without turning her head.

Hayley approached slowly. "Who do I have to speak with?" she asked nervously.

"A friend of mine called Angela Wyatt." Lizzie was busy tapping keys. "You can talk to her in London – there's an eight-hour time difference so it's afternoon over there. It's the only time Angela could find to hook up with us."

Giving up on a last effort to tame her hair, Hayley sat reluctantly beside Lizzie and stared at the screen. "This feels weird," she muttered, "and I have a feeling that I'm gonna say something totally stupid."

"Relax. Angela's easy to talk to. I knew she'd already found a boy from a stunt-riding stables in California, but she's still looking for a girl. She's making a movie here in Colorado so that's why I sent her the training videos of you riding bareback."

"Yeah, I hoped it was something like that," Hayley told Lizzie, feeling a buzz of excitement. This could turn out to be the best summer ever!

"I didn't mention it earlier because I've left it really late and I didn't want to get your hopes up."

"So she's not shooting the movie in England?" Hayley checked as Lizzie tapped more keys and the dial-up tone began.

"No. She's over there to find a lead actor but she'll be back in the States later this week, ready to start shooting."

"What's the story about?" Hayley asked but there was no time for Lizzie to answer before a woman's head and shoulders appeared on screen. Her dark hair was styled into a short bob and she wore a white shirt, and glasses on a chain round her neck.

"Hayley?" the woman asked. "Hi. I'm Angela Wyatt. I've watched the videos of you on that Paint horse—"

"Cool Kid," Hayley broke in then grimaced. "Sorry – I didn't mean to interrupt."

"Yes. Cool Kid looked amazing," Angela carried right on. "And I could tell you were really into riding bareback."

"I love it!" Hayley grinned. Thrown into talking about what she knew best, she forgot about her bed-hair and crumpled T-shirt. "It's a big challenge, don't get me wrong, but I trust Cool Kid with my life. He's the smartest horse ever and he knows never to try anything I can't deal with."

The director nodded. "Enthusiasm and skill, trust between rider and horse – those are the qualities I need for this movie. What I'm specifically looking for is a stunt-riding double for Mercedes Caro – you've heard of her?"

"Heard of her?" Hayley yelped. Mercedes was only the brightest new star in the Hollywood firmament. She had a million followers on Twitter, for goodness' sake!

"Good, well she plays the lead. The movie is called *Pioneer*. Mercedes' character is named Emily Waterson and the narrative is that Emily is the only member of her small family to survive the journey west by wagon trail in the early 1840s."

Hayley listened but her heart was beating fast and she could scarcely take in the avalanche of facts and figures. Auditions usually meant riding in the round pen in front of a casting director, along with three or four competitors for the role – not sweating in a dim, musty tack room and talking to a computer screen.

"The horses pulling the wagon die of thirst in the

desert and Emily's father, mother and baby brother don't make it either. Emily is discovered close to death by a Native American boy named Three Feathers and he takes her on horseback to his village where his father is chief. But the big question is – will the Pueblo Indians accept or reject the orphan girl? For a flavour of what the film will be like, think *Dances with Wolves*."

"Oh, I love that movie!" Hayley cried. It happened to be one of her favourites, mainly because of the horse action and the extreme wilderness settings. Even though the ending made her cry, she reckoned she'd watched the DVD at least twenty times.

"Anyway, that's the major plotline and the setting," Angela rounded off her description. "Do you like the sound of it?"

The question jolted Hayley into a breathless response. "Yeah. Sure. Totally." Jeez, she sounded like a five-year-old. Was that really all she could come up with?

Angela smiled and then went on to stress the high standard she'd set for the job. "Mercedes' double has to be the best teen stunt rider in the business. Her character has to show Three Feathers and his father that she can ride and hunt as well as any of the kids in his tribe, so that they'll accept her and let her stay. Talk to me, Hayley – do you think you're the girl for the job?"

Hayley swallowed hard. Not only would she have to be the best, she also had to convince Angela Wyatt that she could do it. "Just give me and Cool Kid the chance," she replied, her heart still pounding. "You won't be sorry, I swear!"

The director put on her glasses and glanced down at some paperwork on her desk. "I've found a kid called Billy Lindermann to ride for the Three Feathers character and I've looked at plenty of videos of potential girl riders these last two days," she said slowly. "There's one I especially like at Pete Mason's High Noon Stables – a girl called Laura Silverton. I thought I ought to mention that to you, Lizzie, given the circumstances."

Hayley held her breath. She couldn't bear to look in Lizzie's direction when Angela dropped the name of her mean ex-husband. But it turned out she needn't have worried.

"Laura doesn't look quite right for the role. She doesn't have Mercedes' physique. So anyway, in the end she didn't get the job," Angela went on. "Besides,

Lizzie, I've been looking for a way to work with you for a long time. I just needed to be convinced you had the right rider for this role."

"And?" Lizzie prompted. "Do we?"

Angela took off her glasses and looked up, directly into the small camera lens at the top of her screen. "Three things clinched it. First, Hayley, your confidence shines through in your body language and your communication with your horse – I really like that about you."

Hayley nodded and smiled. However, right now, confident was the last thing she felt. She kept her fingers crossed under the desk and she felt her heart knock against her ribs.

"Secondly, plain and simple, I loved that horse!"

Hayley's heart filled with pride for Cool Kid. "Just wait till I tell him," she murmured.

"Thirdly, Lizzie, it was the video sequence of Hayley and Cool Kid loping through the creek that did it for me. The low sun in the west, the long shadows, the sparkling spray – magnificent!"

"Thank you," Lizzie's response was typically modest.

"So, Hayley, you passed your audition with flying

colours," Angela announced. "I want you and your horse on set on Thursday this week, ready to start shooting on Friday. Castle Rock, south-west of Durango – see you there, guys!"

chapter four

As soon as she received the good news, Hayley rushed straight out to the meadow to tell Cool Kid.

"I know, I know - you can't actually understand what I'm saying," she said, her arms around his neck. "But anyway I wanted you to know before anyone else does - Angela Wyatt totally loves you. That's mostly what made up her mind that we're the right team to work on *Pioneer*."

Cool Kid snickered then turned his head to nuzzle her hair. "So long as you're happy then I am, too," he seemed to say.

"It means we'll have to put in a lot more work today," she warned, clipping on his lead rope and walking him to the gate. "We need to be ready for anything Angela asks us to do - agreed?"

He snickered again and pawed the ground, as if to say *Open the gate – let's go!*

"Lizzie says we have to learn backflip dismounts," Hayley continued. "That's where I stand on your back and flip backwards, do one whole mid-air somersault then land on the ground. Then maybe we'll move on to a spot of bareback Roman riding if there's time – we'll need two horses for that, so I'll ask Kellie if we can borrow Dylan. Then who knows what else we'll try to fit in before we leave for Durango first thing tomorrow."

Talking all the while, Hayley led Cool Kid from the meadow into the corral. She didn't notice Alisa, Kami and Kellie standing on the tack-room porch until they suddenly broke out in a loud cheer and a round of applause.

"Congratulations!" Alisa called. "We heard the good news from Lizzie."

"It's so cool!" Kami ran to stroke Cool Kid. "Who's a clever boy? So, so smart!"

Cool Kid took the compliments with a burr of his lips, a toss of his handsome head and flick of his nut-brown forelock.

"I always knew something excellent would turn up."

Kellie's warm smile told Hayley that she was really happy for her.

Hayley handed Cool Kid over to Kami and went to join Kellie and Alisa on the porch. "You're sure you're not sore at me?" she asked them.

They shook their heads. "Why should we be?" Kellie asked.

"Cos you're both awesome riders. Everyone here at Stardust is."

"But you and Cool Kid are better at bareback – no question," Kellie quickly pointed out. "So anyway, I used Lizzie's office computer to look up the *Pioneer* website."

"You did? What did you find out?"

"There's already a heap of pre-publicity out there – interviews with Mercedes Caro and her co-star, Justin Beck, who Angela just signed up for the role of Three Feathers. There's a massive budget for this movie, Hayley. It's going to be huge!"

"Whoa – wait! Rewind. Did you just say Justin Beck?" Hayley gasped. "*The* Justin Beck – the actor from *Moon Mission*?"

"Who else?" Kellie laughed. "The last I heard, there's only one Justin Beck."

Hayley couldn't believe her luck. "He was so hot in that movie, even dressed from head to toe in a clunky spacesuit and moon boots."

"Seriously hot," Alisa agreed, trying to keep a straight face. Then she couldn't help it – she broke into a grin. "What happened to Josh Collier? I thought he was your fave film star?"

"He still is," Hayley insisted. She had the signed T-shirt to prove it. "It's just that I can't believe I'll be on set with Justin Beck." She sighed and clutched both hands to her chest.

"Uh-oh, Doctor Alisa, I'm afraid we have a serious case of hero worship. Hayley is about to faint!" Kellie held out her arms, ready to catch her when she swooned.

"I am not!"

"You so are!"

Blushing, Hayley shoulder-shoved Kellie sideways into Alisa, who made a show of staggering backwards.

"Girls, girls!" Lizzie cried, striding out of the ranch house towards them. When she reached the porch she grabbed Hayley's dusty grey Stetson from a hook behind the door and jammed it on her head. "No time for fooling around. We have work to do."

★ ★ ★ ★ ★

"Now they're saying Mercedes Caro and Justin Beck are an item," Kellie reported during Lizzie and Hayley's lunch break, having checked a Hollywood gossip forum for the latest news.

"Who's 'they'?" Hayley frowned, taking a bite from her sandwich as she let Cool Kid drink from the water barrel in the corral.

"The paparazzi, gossip columnists, celeb-watchers – anyone who's anyone in showbiz."

"Then it's definitely not true," Hayley decided. "Anyway, we don't care, do we, Cool Kid?" All they currently cared about was perfecting the backflip dismount – the hardest thing they'd worked on so far.

"Good but not good enough," Lizzie had told her after the first three attempts at the backflip. The fourth try had elicited a quick nod of the head from the trainer but no comment. Hayley and Cool Kid had focused on every detail they'd been taught so far and performed the stunt a fifth time. Anticlockwise round the pen at a smooth lope for one full circuit, then the transition from sitting to squatting and then the critical leap from the galloping horse and the gravity-defying backflip. Land soundly on two feet, let the horse lope on. Phew!

"Now that," Lizzie had said with a brief, bright-eyed smile, "was as near perfect as it gets!"

"Do you need help with your laundry and packing?" Alisa asked Hayley as Lizzie reappeared from the house, coffee mug in hand. "You know you don't have much time to get ready."

Laundry! Packing! Hayley hadn't even given them a thought. "You're right. My good jeans need to go through the washer and drier, plus my best blue shirt has two missing buttons and I've run out of scrunchies for my hair ... and the stampede string on my hat needs fixing..."

"Jeans, shirt, scrunchies, stampede string ... leave it with me and the girls," Alisa smiled, pushing the frazzled Hayley back into the corral. "Your focus is on learning new stunts."

"Thanks! Roman riding next," Hayley told her hurriedly. "Kellie, is it OK if we borrow Dylan?"

"Sure. He's in the feed stall, getting some extra grain." Kellie ran to fetch him while Hayley led Cool Kid into the round pen for his second training session of the day.

stardust stables

★ ★ ★ ★ ★

"Chill, Hayley."

Ross's well-intentioned comment went unheard as Hayley scrabbled in a dark, dusty corner of the tack room, searching for Cool Kid's best head collar. It had been a long, hot afternoon in the round pen.

"Is this what you're looking for?" he asked.

Hayley emerged from a tangled heap of old lead ropes, her face streaked with dirt, wisps of straw caught in her braided hair. "Where did you find it?"

"Hanging on its hook where it should be," he told her. "Why not come and hang out with the guys at the soda fountain."

"Tempting, but no time," she muttered, taking the head collar from him and trying to ignore another weird heart flutter. The afternoon training session had been exciting and challenging – a mixture of ups and downs. She'd worked hard on the Roman riding to get another smile out of Lizzie and it had only happened after two hours of trying. But at last she'd learned to stand astride Dylan and Cool Kid as they loped in perfect unison round the pen.

Ross studied her as she set about finding Cool Kid's brush and curry comb. "You OK? You look like you're running on empty."

"Yeah, but I still have a million things to do. By the way, have Jack and Becca got back from Alaska yet?"

Ross spotted the brush and comb and handed them to Hayley. "No. When are they due?"

"Their plane should've landed in Denver an hour ago."

"So give them a couple more hours to reload Pepper on to the trailer and drive out here. Erm, Hayley..." Ross hesitated.

"What's up?" She'd bustled from one corner of the tack room to the saddle racks next to the office and was hauling a saddle from its rail. "Just in case it turns out we need it when we're on set," she explained.

"You might want to check that saddle before you clean it," he pointed out.

She looked again then slid it back into place. "Whoops – it's yours. Sorry."

"Come on, chill," he said again. "Why don't you grab Cool Kid's bridle and I'll clean your saddle for you."

"Thanks, but no thanks." Hayley was determined to do the preparation herself and still finish in time for dinner. She stopped just long enough to look directly into his clear grey eyes. "Really, Ross – I'm fine."

He nodded and backed slowly out of the door. "So see you later?"

She nodded and blushed. "See you."

"You're sure you don't need any help?"

"I'm sure." Why was he hovering, and was it just the low sun on his face or was he blushing, too?

"Bye," he said as he finally disappeared from sight.

"Hi," said Kellie, appearing two seconds later with a big grin on her face. "I saw that!"

"What? There was nothing to see."

"Says you!" Kellie cried. "Wait till I tell the others – Ross has developed one huge crush on you!"

"He has not!" Hayley set about rubbing the dust from Cool Kid's saddle.

"Has!"

"Has not!" *No way, not possible*, she told herself. And even if it was true, she had no time right now to think about it! Instead she spat on her duster then rubbed and polished until the tooled leather shone.

★ ★ ★ ★ ★

"Guess what – Ross has a crush on Hayley!" Kellie announced to Alisa and Kami when she found them doing Hayley's laundry. "I just saw them together in the tack room."

"Swee-eet!" Kami's eyes lit up as she sewed new buttons on to Hayley's blue shirt.

"You could see that coming a mile away," Alisa said. "The way Ross goes quiet whenever Hayley's around and blushes when anyone mentions her name."

"I never noticed." Kellie looked puzzled. "Then again, I guess I wasn't looking."

"Shh, here comes the boss!" Kami warned as she glanced out of the door and noticed Lizzie heading towards their bunkhouse.

Lizzie spotted the girls in the laundry and changed direction. Her face looked serious as she came into the room and showed them her iPad. "Check this out," she said. "Becca called me en route from the airport and told me to look at the High Noon website. This is what I found."

Kami, Kellie and Alisa crowded round the small

screen. Pete Mason's home page featured a box containing a newsflash: "High Noon stunt rider gets major role in blockbuster movie!"

"Read on," Lizzie urged, scrolling down.

"'*Pioneer*'..." Kami said out loud.

"'Laura Silverton... Mercedes Caro... Justin Beck'," Kellie read. "Hey, this can't be right!"

"No, it can't, because Hayley just got that job," Alisa agreed. "What's Pete Mason playing at?"

"He's twisting things as usual," Lizzie told them. "When you scroll right down to the bottom, it turns out that Laura hasn't got the leading stunt-riding role, in spite of what it looks like at the top of the page."

"It does say 'major role'," Kami pointed out.

"I know, but what it comes down to is that Angela has recruited Laura to work on the movie but not as Mercedes Caro's double. In reality, she'll be one of a bunch of riders used in crowd scenes."

"Phew." For a second Kellie was relieved but then she thought ahead. "Jeez, that means Mason and Lucy will most likely be in Durango when you and Hayley are there."

"I sure hope he doesn't try and spoil things for you,"

Alisa sighed. No one at Stardust liked Lizzie's ex and his underhand tricks.

Lizzie sighed and nodded. "What do you think – shall I tell Hayley now or wait until we get there?"

"Tell her now," Kami and Kellie said straight away.

"Wait," Alisa argued. "Have you seen her lately? She's hyper. If you land this problem on her now, before she goes to bed, she won't get any sleep at all."

Lizzie nodded. "OK, we don't say anything at supper and we tell Becca not to mention it when she gets here. Alisa's right – we need Hayley to be rested and ready for tomorrow's drive. Agreed?"

chapter five

It turned out that Lizzie needn't have worried about Becca spilling the beans because it was past midnight before Jack finally drove the trailer along the moonlit road and down into the valley where Stardust Stables nestled alongside Elk Creek. By that time, Hayley was safely tucked up in bed, though not asleep.

"Do I hear the trailer?" she whispered anxiously to Alisa.

Alisa's bed was nearest to the window so she sat up and peered through the gap in the curtains. "Yep, that's Jack with Becca and Pepper – home at last, thank goodness."

"What kept them so long?" Hayley wondered. One of the reasons she'd lain awake was that Jack and Becca hadn't shown up in time for dinner.

"Jack called to say the trailer tyre blew out," said Alisa. "Apparently he had to wait an hour and a half for the rescue service to come and fix it. That's what Ross told me anyhow. I'd have passed it on to you, only I thought you were asleep."

"Bad news about the tyre, but at least it's fixed and it means we've got the transport we need to take us to Durango." Sighing, Hayley turned on to her side and pulled the blankets higher. "I was freaking out back there," she admitted from under her covers.

"It turned out OK, so stop worrying," Alisa advised.

There was silence for a while then Hayley said, "How many pairs of jeans did I pack?"

"Three," Alisa told her. "Plus three shirts."

"Did I pack my boots?"

"No, because you'll be wearing them for the journey. Likewise your denim jacket."

Silence again then, "Stampede string!"

"Fixed," Alisa reminded her with a yawn. "Kami did it for you. Just chill, OK."

"I'll try," Hayley promised. But her legs were twitchy and eventually she had to stand up in the dark and stretch them. "Sorry," she whispered.

There was no answer from a sleeping Alisa.

What is wrong with me, Hayley wondered. What had happened to Hayley Forest, the laid-back joker? How come she was so uptight all of a sudden?

"Because," she told herself as she crept back into bed and pulled the covers over her head, "this is the biggest movie by far that Cool Kid and I have ever got to work on and who knows – with Mercedes Caro and Justin Beck starring, it'll probably turn out to be the biggest blockbusting movie of the decade. No wonder I'm scared!"

"So, good luck with the bareback riding," Jack told Hayley as she led Cool Kid into the trailer at 6.30 next morning. "Not that you'll need it, from what Lizzie tells me."

He was up early despite the late-night emergency on the road home from Denver, checking that she and Lizzie had everything they needed.

"Thanks." Now that the day had arrived, Hayley felt just the right level of excitement mixed in with the jitters she'd been experiencing over the last twenty-four hours.

Her mind was alert as she climbed up into the cab beside Lizzie.

"It's a good day for the drive." Jack noted the clear blue sky. "They say the temperature shouldn't rise above eighty-five degrees Fahrenheit, even down in Durango – not too hot for Cool Kid to be cooped up in the back of the trailer."

"Yeah, and Hayley and I will have plenty to talk about on the road." Lizzie started the engine.

Frown lines appeared on Jack's handsome face. "You mean Pete Mason?"

"What about him?" Hayley wanted to know. The very name set off alarm bells in her head.

"I'll tell you once we're on the road," Lizzie promised.

"Drive carefully," Jack told her, stepping back to let her ease the trailer out of the yard. He gave a wave then strode into the barn as Alisa, Kellie and Kami burst out of the bunkhouse in their PJs.

"Good luck!" they called, waving both arms and whooping. Ross, Tom and Zak joined them from the boys' bunkhouse and added to the raucous yelling. "Go, girl! Go, Hayley!"

Hayley smiled to herself and felt a warm glow when

she heard Ross's voice rise above the rest.

"You're getting quite a send-off," Lizzie grinned.

Hayley leaned out of the cab to wave back. "But what's this thing about Pete Mason?" she insisted as the trailer climbed the hill.

"Nothing much." Lizzie had decided to underplay her concerns. "He'll be on set with one of his riders, that's all."

"Oh, great." Hayley recalled how Mason had tried to claim half of their horses as his own then stampeded the whole herd out of the meadow in a fit of pique. He was a nasty piece of work, no doubt about it.

"The girl's name is Laura Silverton. Remember, Angela said she auditioned her for the role you got? Other than that, I don't know anything about her," Lizzie admitted.

"Let's hope she's easier to get along with than her boss," Hayley muttered.

"Hopefully they won't get in our way. Now, time for you to sit back and relax." Lizzie offered Hayley some gum. "Everyone knows about Justin Beck but fill me in on what I need to know about Mercedes Caro so I don't make a fool of myself when we get there. What movies should I have seen her in? What makes her so special? Are we going to like her, and more especially is she going to like working with us or will she be too stuck up to even notice?"

After an hour's smooth ride along the Interstate, Hayley and Lizzie had relaxed into the long journey south. There'd been no sound from Cool Kid in the back of the trailer, which meant he was happy munching hay and dozing.

Hayley read the exit sign for Colorado Springs then began to look out for a turn-off to Pagosa Springs, where a famous horse trainer was based. She and Lizzie passed the time by talking about his natural methods of training colts and how much they hated the bad old ways of breaking them in.

"Just the words – 'breaking in'," Hayley pointed out. "Why did anyone ever think you needed to use force to gain a horse's trust – hobbling and sacking out, all that horrible stuff?"

"Some people still do, unfortunately," Lizzie said. She had her attention on the road and Hayley saw her stiffen slightly as a large vehicle edged out of a small side road on to the highway, forcing her to brake. "Road hog," she muttered under her breath.

"'High Noon Stables'." Hayley squinted to read a wooden sign that pointed down the narrow dirt road. "So that must be Pete Mason's trailer ahead of us?"

"Yeah – and that's a typical piece of bad behaviour from my wonderful ex. Oh and check this out ahead – now he decides to slow down and pull into the side of the freeway, which is totally illegal." Exasperated, Lizzie indicated and pulled wide of Mason's slowing vehicle, giving Hayley the chance to study the high-sided silver trailer with its scarlet High Noon logo emblazoned on the side. She glimpsed a stocky guy in a black baseball cap at the wheel and in the passenger seat a girl with short dark hair and hooped silver earrings, wearing a denim jacket with its collar turned up. "Laura Silverton," she reminded herself quietly.

"At least we know he'll definitely be there at the same time as us – it's best to be prepared," Lizzie sighed, trying to put Mason out of her mind by turning on the radio. "We'll take a break soon," she promised. "Coffee, ice cream – whatever you like."

stardust stables

★★★★★

"One scoop of chocolate and one strawberry." Hayley gave her order over the counter at Betsy's Diner. "With chocolate sauce, please."

Lizzie had pulled off the road into a wide, gravel-covered parking area. They'd checked that Cool Kid was still OK in the back of the trailer, given him fresh water then come into the small, old-fashioned diner with its red leatherette bench seats and vases of artificial flowers set out next to ketchup bottles in the centre of neatly laid tables.

"Anything to drink?" the waitress asked Hayley.

"OJ," Hayley decided. She chose a table by the window while Lizzie ordered coffee and a chicken sandwich. It was from here that Hayley saw another driver pull off the road and quickly recognized the High Noon trailer as it parked alongside theirs. "Uh-oh," she warned Lizzie, who had just carried their food across. "Here comes trouble."

Lizzie tutted and shook her head. They both pretended to study the menu as Mason and Laura left the trailer and headed for the diner.

But Lizzie's ex wasn't about to let them ignore him. "Look who's here!" he exclaimed, taking off his cap and throwing it down on the table next to theirs.

Hayley noticed that he hadn't shaved recently, and decided that designer stubble wasn't really his best look.

"Well, Lizzie – who'd have thought we'd be working together on this movie." Mason put on a big cheesy grin to match his loud, fake-friendly voice before sending Laura to order coffee at the counter.

Lizzie shrugged. "I wouldn't call it working together, exactly."

"But then I should've realized one of your riders would land a job on this movie because you and Angela go way back, don't you?"

Lizzie bristled and met his gaze for the first time. "Hayley got this job on merit, not for any other reason."

"You would say that, wouldn't you?" Mason sneered. He didn't thank Laura as she came back with his drink. "You forgot the cream," he snapped.

Blushing, Laura went back to the counter, casting a shy look at Hayley as she passed by their table.

Lizzie found she couldn't let the insult pass. "I'm not

just saying it. It's absolutely true. You won't find a better bareback rider than Hayley anywhere."

Mason's laugh was as fake as his smile. "You wait till you see my girl ride. It's in her blood – I mean, literally in her blood. She's part Navajo on her mother's side. You can't learn to ride bareback the way Laura does – you're born with it, it's in your DNA."

No need to broadcast it to the whole world, Hayley thought as Laura came back with Mason's jug of cream. Other customers in the diner were staring at her and she obviously hated the attention.

By this time, Lizzie had had enough of her loud-mouthed ex. "You finished your ice cream?" she checked with Hayley, who nodded. "Then let's go."

Thank goodness! Once outside the diner, Hayley inhaled a breath of fresh air. She followed Lizzie across the car park back to the trailer, only pausing to check in on Cool Kid once more before jumping into the cab, taking her hat from the seat, putting it on and pulling the brim low over her forehead.

"Is your horse doing OK?" Lizzie checked.

"Yeah, he's cool. I noticed you didn't finish your sandwich back there."

Lizzie took her own deep breath once she'd eased out on to the road. "Suddenly I wasn't hungry," she commented, following the sign south to Durango.

They drove for two more hours, bypassing Durango city centre before Lizzie warned Hayley to look out for a temporary sign that would direct them to their destination. "It'll say 'Sunset Films' – that's the name of the production company. Angela says the sign is small and not very noticeable. The track doesn't have a name for the satnav to pick up but it comes roughly twenty miles west of town."

Hayley leaned forward in her seat, keeping her eyes peeled as they drove on along a bare, winding road with only an occasional flat-roofed, adobe-style house set back under sparse pinon pine trees. In the distance and to either side of the road, she saw towers of red sandstone rock rising like giant fingers from flat horizons.

"Different from back home, huh?" Lizzie commented. "This area isn't named Four Corners for nothing."

"Four Corners?" Hayley asked.

"Yeah – it's where the borders of New Mexico,

Arizona, Utah and Colorado come together. We're on the edge of the Mesa Verde, the area where the Pueblo tribes constructed their amazing cliff dwellings."

"Wait – we're here!" Hayley cried suddenly when she spotted the makeshift Sunset Films sign.

Lizzie braked and signalled to turn left while waiting for a guy on an oncoming Harley-Davidson bike to cruise by. Then she eased on to a track too narrow to be called a road, glancing at her overhead mirror and noticing that they weren't alone. She bit her lip and said nothing to Hayley.

But Hayley heard the rumble of a truck engine and looked into the wing mirror to spot Mason close behind. "He's tailgating us," she complained. "Why is he doing that? Is he crazy?"

Lizzie concentrated hard on the road ahead. "Don't worry – he can't go anywhere in a hurry. It's too narrow for him to overtake."

"And he can't possibly see more than a couple of metres ahead of him. We're raising too much dust." By now Hayley was seriously worried. Mason was pushing them on faster than they wanted to go, so that their trailer bumped and swayed along the twisting, uneven track.

"Wait, I can see a passing place ahead – I'm going to pull over," Lizzie decided. She braked, indicated and swung the trailer left.

Behind them, they heard Mason slam on his brakes. His front fender clipped them as he squeezed by.

"Insane!" Hayley muttered. She felt the right wheels of their trailer dip into a shallow gulley to the side of the road then heard a loud, sharp bang followed by a sudden jolt and a further tilt to the right. "Jeez, what was that? It sounded like a gunshot!"

"No, I think we blew another tyre!" Lizzie gasped, opening her door and jumping out.

Hayley opened her own door then half tumbled out of the cab into the dry gulley. She ran straight to the back of the trailer and jumped up on the fender to look through the window and check that Cool Kid was safe. What she saw came as another big shock. Her beloved horse lay on his side in the straw, legs flailing as he tried to get up. His eyes rolled and he let out a high-pitched squeal of fear.

"Cool Kid!" She wrenched the handle then flung open the door.

Just at that moment, Cool Kid managed to shift his

weight and fold his legs under him. He raised himself on to his knees and with a lurch he was back on his feet.

"It's OK," Hayley told him, stepping up into the trailer and trying to keep her voice calm as she went forward and took hold of his head collar. She could see how scared he was – ears flat against his head, teeth bared and eyes still rolling wildly. "Cool Kid, I'm here. It's me. You're going to be fine."

"Watch out, bikes coming!" Lizzie yelled from outside the trailer.

There was a roar of engines, then two motorbikes passed so close that the grit kicked up by their tyres rattled against the trailer's metal sides. The noise ratcheted Cool Kid's anxiety level up another few notches so that he reared away from Hayley, who lost hold of his head collar. His front hooves came down with a loud, hollow clatter.

"Another bike coming!" Lizzie warned, her voice almost drowned out by the roaring engine.

Out of his mind with fear as the third Harley-Davidson passed by, Cool Kid kicked out with his back feet, which thudded against the sides of the trailer. Then, with a powerful thrust from his haunches he launched himself forward towards the exit.

"Stop!" Hayley cried. She had to press herself to the side of the trailer as he stampeded past. "Lizzie, stop him – he's going crazy in here!"

Too late. Cool Kid saw the square of light; the escape route from the ordeal he'd just been through. He had only one idea in his head – to get out of there.

His hooves clattered on the metal floor then he burst out of the trailer, stumbling as he landed in the shallow gulley. He went down on to his front knees and up again.

Hayley and Lizzie ran after him but he was too fast for them. Back on his feet, he reared up, mane swinging back, nostrils flared. Then down and on, away from the nightmare trailer, up on to the track, veering off and cutting diagonally up the hillside, kicking up red dirt, making for the refuge of some nearby Douglas fir trees.

"Stop!" Hayley called after him. She was trembling and her heart thudded against her ribs as she saw him disappear. "Cool Kid, please, come back!"

chapter six

Cool Kid fled and Hayley followed.

Without waiting for Lizzie she set off towards the trees at a sprint, which soon slowed to a laboured run as she hit a patch of soft red earth. For every metre she travelled, she lost ground by sinking and sliding backwards, struggling to keep her balance on the shifting surface. When she realized she was being overtaken by two women on mountain bikes she slowed to a halt. By this time there was no sign of Cool Kid in amongst the trees.

One of the women, dressed in cycling shorts, sports sunglasses, a white helmet and bright yellow top, stopped just ahead of her. "What happened?" she asked.

"My horse," Hayley gasped. "He freaked out and

escaped from his trailer. I have to find him and bring him back."

"You want us to take a look in that stand of pine trees for you?" the other woman asked.

"Yes – no!" Quickly, Hayley changed her mind. The mountain bikers would get there before her but they might scare Cool Kid into fleeing even further. "Can I borrow a bike?"

The first woman nodded while the second turned to speak with Lizzie, who was struggling up the hill after Hayley. "There's a trail ten metres to the left," she explained to Hayley. "The ground is firmer – you'll get up to there faster."

Gratefully Hayley grabbed the bike and found the trail. She sweated as she covered the two-hundred-metre stretch, finally reaching the shade of the trees where she decided to abandon the bike and enter on foot. "Cool Kid!" she called, as her eyes slowly adjusted to the shadows. She stopped, listened for an answer but heard nothing. She walked on then called again.

Wait – what was that? Was something stirring deep in the middle of the stand of trees? Hayley sensed a living, breathing creature close by. She heard a rustle through long, dry grass, held her breath and took a step towards the noise.

A pair of yellow eyes stared out of the darkness, then another and another. With a sharp intake of breath Hayley drew back.

Three grey, skinny shapes, hackles raised, emerged stealthily from between the tall trees. The creatures were smaller than wolves but bigger than foxes.

Coyotes! Hayley gasped as she backed up against a thick, rough trunk. They kept her fixed in their gaze as they stopped, savage jaws open, tongues lolling. For what seemed like an age, there was complete stillness. Then Lizzie approached the trees on a second borrowed bike, flinging it to the ground and running through sagebrush into the dense shadows. The three coyotes turned their heads sharply towards her then whipped round and swiftly retreated the way they'd come.

"Anything?" Lizzie gasped when she found Hayley.

"Coyotes – three of them," Hayley whispered. There were probably more, a whole pack, hidden in the long grass, lying low until the intruders left.

"Jeez, are you OK?" Lizzie checked.

"I'm fine," Hayley assured her, taking a deep breath to steady her nerves.

"No sign of Cool Kid?"

Hayley had no time to answer before one of the cyclists arrived on foot and broke in on their conversation. "We just saw something run out the far side of the trees, up on to the high ridge," she told them breathlessly. "Too big for a deer. What colour is your horse?"

"He's brown and white," Hayley told her.

The cyclist nodded. "Then it was definitely him. Come and take a look."

"Which ridge?" Hayley asked as they followed the woman out of the trees on to the sun-baked, open mountainside. Once more their eyes needed time to adjust and by the time they could finally make out the rocky horizon and follow their guide's pointing finger, there was no horse to be seen.

"Which way did he go?" Lizzie asked the second mountain biker who waited by a tall, prickly pear cactus, her hand raised to her eyes to shield them from the sun.

"Something set him off again. He disappeared over

the far side of the ridge," the woman reported.

"Come on, let's follow him!" Hayley told Lizzie.

"No." Lizzie held her back. "There's no point."

"What do you mean?" Frantically Hayley pulled herself free and tried to set off towards the ridge.

"Cool Kid is faster than us – he's going to outrun us every time."

"So we're giving up?" Hayley couldn't believe her ears. She felt hot tears sting her eyes. "He's out there all alone and he doesn't have a clue where he is. We can't just leave him!"

"We're not going to leave him," Lizzie assured her, gazing up at the empty, scorched horizon. "We're going to regroup and get some help."

"From where?" Hayley looked around desperately, seeing four hikers with backpacks coming down a trail on the opposite side of the valley. She heard another Harley-Davidson approaching from the direction of the highway. Hikers, cyclists and bikers – what use were they in their search for the spooked horse?

"Help from the movie set," Lizzie decided.

"And how do we get there?" Hayley pointed to their abandoned trailer stuck deep in the gulley.

"We walk," came the firm reply. "I reckon it's less than a mile down the dirt track. They'll have rough-terrain vehicles and plenty of people to join in the search."

Hayley shook her head. "Cool Kid could be miles away by the time we organize a search party. Then it'll be nightfall and he'll still be all alone. There are coyotes out here – I just saw them."

"It's all we can do," Lizzie said. "We'll walk to the film set and hopefully find a satellite signal. I'll call Jack and tell him what happened. Then we'll borrow a Jeep and scour the area, cover as much ground as we can before sunset."

Hayley and Lizzie trudged wearily along the dirt road, desperate to reach the movie set. They came across mule deer – two does and a baby – nibbling at tender shoots of sagebrush. At the sound of Hayley and Lizzie's approaching footsteps, they raised their heads and bounded up the parched hillside. Small collared lizards sunbathed on hot rocks by the roadside while a keen-eyed eagle soared overhead.

"What's that ahead of us?" Hayley asked as they

rounded a bend in the road. The land dipped away in front of them and a broad river snaked through the valley, shining silver in the sunlight.

"It's the Animas River," Lizzie replied. "And look – there are trailers and tents under the junipers on the near bank. That must be the Sunset team."

"At last!" Hayley picked up speed on the downhill slope, taking a shortcut through thorn bushes and cacti that scratched and pricked her bare arms. As Hayley drew close to the nearest trailer and Lizzie went off in search of Angela Wyatt, she saw a man sitting on metal steps leading up to an open door so she raised her arms to attract his attention. "Hi," she yelled. "You didn't see a runaway horse by any chance?"

The guy, who was in his thirties, with long fair hair and wearing a white T-shirt, jeans and cowboy boots, got up and came to meet her. "Hard to say. There are forty or fifty horses on site. What does yours look like?"

"He's a brown and white Paint," Hayley gasped, wiping sweat from her forehead.

"So come and take a look," he invited, leading the way behind a big canvas marquee towards an enclosure containing the Sunset horses. "By the way,

I'm Tyler Miller. I act as wrangler on the *Pioneer* set."

"I'm Hayley Forest."

"Yeah, you're Mercedes' stunt double," he stated without surprise. "Angela showed me your audition video."

"That's me."

He stopped and gave her a quizzical, sympathetic look. "So you lost your horse?"

"There was an accident with our trailer a mile back. Cool Kid freaked out and ran off."

"And you're hoping he made his way down here to join our remuda?" Tyler stood aside to give Hayley a better chance to inspect the enclosure. "As you can see, we have a lot of Paints."

She studied the horses milling around a metal feeder containing alfalfa, spotting at least half a dozen black and white Paints and an equal number with the same colouring as Cool Kid. On top of that there were sorrels, bays and Appaloosas.

"Well?" Tyler asked. "Is he here?"

As Hayley sighed and shook her head, the person she least wanted to see walked over from the big marquee.

"Problem?" Pete Mason asked with an uneasy grin.

"Hayley's horse went missing," Tyler told him.

Still looking uneasy, Mason turned down the corners of his mouth. "That Cool Kid, he always was a handful, even way back when I was co-owner of the Stardust outfit. He spooks at every little thing and he's a real Houdini, an escape artist like you wouldn't believe."

Hayley shook her head. "That's not true," she muttered. She could see what Mason was playing at – his plan was to wrongfoot her and her horse in order to draw attention away from the part his terrible driving had played in the recent accident. But there was no time to argue with him, since Lizzie came hurrying up with the director, Angela Wyatt.

"I called Jack and told him what happened to the trailer," Lizzie told Hayley with a meaningful look in Mason's direction. "He reckons it's the same tyre that blew on the road home from Denver, which means the repair guy didn't do a good job. Jack's pretty mad about that."

"Such bad luck," Angela sighed, raising her shades and perching them on top of her head. She didn't seem to know about the part Mason's bad driving had played and Hayley knew it would be typical of Lizzie not to dish the dirt even in a situation like this.

Instead, Lizzie stuck to the positive. "I say we're pretty sure to find Cool Kid before nightfall, just so long as we can borrow a vehicle and a couple of guys to help us search."

"Count me in," Tyler said before she'd finished her sentence. "And I'll find Jay Stevens. We can use his Jeep. Meet us outside the catering tent in five."

"Good thinking." Angela gave Hayley a sympathetic smile as Tyler ran off. "And nice to meet you in person, by the way. Looking forward to working with you as soon as we find your horse. Jay and Tyler both know this Mesa Verde territory inside out. If anyone can find your runaway horse, they sure can."

"You did check Cool Kid didn't make it here?" Lizzie gestured towards the crowded enclosure, deliberately turning her back on Mason to talk to Hayley.

"Yeah," said Hayley, running her eye over the herd for a second time, but to no avail. "I guess he's still out there," she sighed.

"Try the river," Mason broke in. "Go figure - sooner or later a thirsty horse will head for water."

"Thanks for the advice," Lizzie muttered, brushing past him as she hurried off to meet the guys with the Jeep. Hayley admired her dignity and her way of rising above the situation.

"Just trying to help," Mason shrugged. He stepped in front of Angela. "Oh and by the way, I didn't plan for this to happen but it turns out that my girl, Laura, could step in here. We've brought along a brown and white Paint from High Noon. His name's Chico, just in case the worst comes to the worst and you need a top horse and rider team to take the place of Hayley and Cool Kid."

chapter seven

"That is not going to happen!" Lizzie vowed as the search party set off with Jay Stevens, a screenwriter on the movie, at the wheel. She hadn't seen the point of making a scene when her ex had made his sneaky offer, but now she was extra determined to find Cool Kid and bring him back safe and sound.

"Shall we check out the river first, like Pete said?" Tyler asked Hayley.

She shrugged. "I'm not sure. The last sighting we had, he was up on a ridge overlooking the movie set."

"That's Truth Overlook. So you want to search the territory on the far side of the ridge?"

"Honestly, I don't know. Lizzie, what do you think?"

"River," she decided. It hurt to admit it, but her ex had a point – horses were drawn to water like iron filings to a magnet.

So Jay followed the rough track along the river bank, pointing out likely spots for a runaway horse to take refuge. "My guess is that he'll stick to open spaces, not get himself boxed in down any narrow gulches or in among trees and bushes. That way he can keep a look out for predators."

"Good thinking," Lizzie agreed. "You know about horses, Jay?"

"Me? No, I just write the script," he laughed. "I make a living sitting behind a desk making up stories out of thin air. Hold on to your hats!" he exclaimed as he braked suddenly, causing his passengers to lurch forward in their seats. "There's a slow-moving pedestrian ahead," he explained with an apologetic smile.

Tyler was the first to spot the snake that had stopped in its tracks and was raising its triangular head towards the Jeep. "Rattlesnake," he told Hayley and Lizzie.

First coyotes, now rattlesnakes – how many more enemies did poor Cool Kid have to contend with out here, Hayley wondered.

"Jay here was born in Durango," Tyler said as they waited for the snake to cross the track. Only when it had slithered into the tall dry grass at the roadside did Jay set off again. "He's lived near to the Mesa Verde for most of his life, so he knows the area better than anyone."

Hayley was already starting to give up on the thirsty-horse theory so she jumped on this new fact. "So which direction would a runaway horse take, if not the river?"

Jay, who was an older guy of forty-five or fifty with short grey hair and a goatee beard, gave the question a lot of thought. "Hard to say," he said at last. "Horses are herd animals, like deer. They like to stick together. And I did hear there are now wild horses out here on the edge of the national park. They came in from Arizona – mustangs, I guess."

"But you can't pinpoint exactly where, I bet," said Lizzie. "Those wild herds move around to find fresh grazing – here one day, twenty miles away the next."

"Yeah, but the park rangers normally keep an eye on them. We could give them a call," Jay suggested, putting on the brakes as the riverside track they were following came to an end.

"I'll do it." Tyler took out his phone.

In the back of the Jeep, Hayley closed her eyes

and took a deep breath. The adults were so sensible and sounded so calm, while she felt desperate and helpless. "Let me climb on to that ledge and take a look downriver," she said to Lizzie, jumping out of the vehicle then scrambling up a nearby rock. The climb was steeper and harder than she'd expected – almost vertical at one point – so she had to find footholds and pick her way carefully up to the ledge. Once she was there, she paused for breath and took in the view.

At this point in its meandering course, the Animas River rolled broad and slow through the valley. Hayley could see a long way ahead, across a flat plain scattered with cacti, yucca and thorn bushes towards the strange rock formations – massive, misshapen fingers of red sandstone – that they'd noticed on their way in. With the sun slowly setting behind them, the bluffs cast long, deep shadows across the empty desert. *There's nothing here for Cool Kid to eat*, she thought with a sinking heart.

"Any sign of him?" Lizzie called.

Hayley sighed and shook her head.

By the time she climbed down from the ledge, Tyler had ended his call to the park rangers.

"Wild mustangs were last spotted out by Mule Deer Lake, about five miles west of here," he reported.

Lizzie narrowed her eyes. "Five miles is not that far, but would Cool Kid make it before nightfall?" she said, thinking out loud. "And would he even know that there were horses out in that direction? Sure, he might pick up tracks and follow them, but wouldn't he rather make his way to the movie set once he's had time to get over his panic and calm down? Isn't that more likely?"

"You want to rely on him realizing that there are other horses like him here on set?" Jay asked.

"He's a smart horse," Lizzie replied. "Plus, we're losing daylight – it'll be dark in under an hour."

Tyler picked up her meaning. "And what would be the point of us staying out here to continue the search?"

As Hayley listened, her heart hit rock bottom and she found herself in a dark, lonely place. She couldn't bear to go back and wait for Cool Kid to show up. She needed to be out searching until the last glimmer of light faded from the landscape. "We can't just give in," she said for the second time that day. Her voice caught in her throat and she had to swallow back tears.

"Going back to base is not giving in." As before,

Lizzie took a firm line. "It's the smartest thing to do right now."

"But..." Hayley's protest ended in a sigh. Her throat was still tight as she pictured Cool Kid trapped overnight down a narrow gully, cowering against a cliff face, surrounded by the pack of wild dogs they'd disturbed earlier. Night time was when coyotes went on the prowl, creeping up on unsuspecting prey by the light of the moon – grey, silent creatures with razor-sharp fangs and glaring, yellow eyes.

"Lizzie's right," Tyler decided as Jay turned the Jeep round.

Hayley bit her lip and endured the drive back to Sunset in silence. By the time the trailers and tents of the film company came into sight, it was almost dark.

"No luck?" Pete Mason was the first on the scene when Jay drew to a halt outside the catering tent. He didn't even try to hide his satisfaction.

Lizzie got out of the car and slammed the door behind her, striding away from her gloating ex in silence. Hayley gave him a wide berth too, walking with her head down and almost bumping into a group of people emerging from the tent, coffee cups in hand.

"Sorry," she mumbled without looking up.

"Hey, aren't you my stunt double?" A girl's voice made Hayley pause and turn round. "That's right – it's me, Mercedes Caro. Don't look so surprised."

Hayley's jaw dropped – she couldn't help it. It turned out that the actress was as stunning in real life as she was on screen. Dressed in fancy, tooled leather boots and denim shorts, her slim legs went on forever. Her belt had a huge silver buckle studded with turquoise to match a chunky necklace and her dark hair was swept into a high ponytail. "Yeah," Hayley admitted, glancing down at her dusty jeans and workaday boots. "Don't worry – I scrub up better than this."

"Hey, no problem." Mercedes took her to one side. "It's Hayley, isn't it? I heard you went looking for your missing horse," she said quietly. "Did you find him?"

Hayley shook her head and her mouth fell open a second time when she realised that Justin Beck was also part of the group that lingered outside the tent. He stood with his back towards her, chatting to Laura Silverton, who glanced uneasily at Hayley. "No, we didn't see any sign of Cool Kid," she told Mercedes. "We're hoping he'll sense there are other horses down here and he'll want to join them now that it's dark."

Mercedes frowned at the news. "Poor you. I know how you must feel."

"You do?"

"Sure. I have my own horse on our family ranch in Texas. Cool Kid probably means everything to you." She leaned in and lowered her voice. "Listen, Hayley – you do know what that Pete Mason guy is saying?"

"That his horse and rider will take our place?"

Mercedes nodded. "The truth is, unless you find Cool Kid by the time we start filming your scene, it could actually happen. I heard Mason discussing it with Angela and she's the first to realize that if we fall behind schedule, it hits the budget big time. Plus, timing's already tight."

"How come?" Hayley asked, her eyes glued on Justin's gorgeous back.

"Angela flew Justin out here for a limited number of days. By this time next week he has to be back in England shooting the movie that they pulled him off to do *Pioneer*."

"Gotcha," Hayley murmured.

"Anyhow, Justin's stunt double – Billy Lindermann –

he doesn't get here until midday. You're due to shoot your first scene together tomorrow evening. I thought you should know."

"Thanks." Hayley had thought she couldn't feel any worse than she already did but the conversation with Mercedes had plunged her further into despair. Needing to be by herself, she turned to walk away from the artificial lights and the groups of people hanging out around the catering tent towards the darkness of the river.

"I really hope you find your horse," Mercedes called after her.

"Thanks," she said again sadly.

She reached the river and gazed down at the slowly flowing water then up at the crescent moon and star-studded sky. There was no wind but there was a chill in the air. Black water slapped against the rocky bank then swirled into small eddies and flowed on.

After a while, the buzz of the phone in Hayley's pocket told her that a text message had come through. She wanted to ignore it, to be alone out here with her thoughts. But it might be news from Lizzie about Cool Kid so she took the phone from her pocket and read the message.

It was from Ross. "Hey, Hayley. We heard about C K. Did u find him yet?"

She thought of her friends back at Stardust, gathered around the soda fountain after a hard day's training with Jack, or doing laundry, or reading and watching videos in the bunk rooms. And here she was in this lonely desert place. Cool Kid was missing and she didn't have anyone to talk to.

"Not yet," she texted back. "Went after him but no luck so far. Really freaking me out. Any ideas about what I should do?"

chapter eight

As Hayley was getting ready for bed in the small tent she'd been assigned for her short stay on location, Ross called her to discuss the bad news.

"I'm so sorry, Hayley – this sucks," he began in a voice that sounded far off and troubled.

Hayley rushed to fill in the details. "Don't I know it? And it's down to Pete Mason. We had to pull the trailer over to let him pass because he was driving like a maniac. We ended up in a ditch and got a flat. Cool Kid couldn't keep his footing – he fell over, and it was awful seeing him try to get up. Then these three guys on Harleys came past and everything got a hundred times worse. Jeez, Ross – it's a nightmare!"

"I've discussed it with the others," he sympathized. "Kellie and Kami say to hope he'll come down of his own accord."

"That's what Lizzie says too."

"Alisa is convinced Cool Kid's survival instinct will kick in."

Hayley sat down on the edge of her steel camp bed. "But there are coyotes out here, and rattlesnakes, plus a bunch of wild mustangs roaming free - what if he gets in among them?"

"You're scared he might join their herd?"

"Exactly. What horse wouldn't be tempted by that kind of freedom - out on the prairie with his new buddies, foraging and living like horses were originally meant to live?"

"Not Cool Kid," Ross insisted. "You and he, you've got an unbelievable bond - he'll come back to you. Anyway, I wanted to say we're all thinking of you - me, Kami, Becca, Kellie, Alisa, and the other guys, too."

"Thanks, Ross." His kindness brought tears to Hayley's eyes and she suddenly felt exhausted.

"Get some sleep, huh?"

"Yeah. I need an early start."

"Promise to call us when you have some news?"

"I will. Bye." Wearily Hayley ended the call and

crawled under her duvet. She lay awake for a long time, staring out through the tent flap at the stars. Then at last she drifted off to sleep and one of the worst days of her life finally came to an end.

She slept longer than planned. The sun was already rising over the San Juan Mountains and the film crew was up, ready to shoot an early morning scene between Mercedes and Justin. Hayley skipped her shower, threw on some clothes and sprinted from her tent to find Lizzie talking with Angela under the awning outside the catering tent. Tyler was there, too, with Pete Mason and Laura.

"No sign of Cool Kid?" Hayley checked with the wrangler, who stood back from the rest of the group.

"Not so far," he reported, indicating with a tilt of his head that she should listen in to the conversation between Mason and the director.

"So I'm offering you the obvious solution to the problem." Mason's voice overrode the others. "This is a big scene. Everything is set up for the point in the narrative where your two major characters first meet.

Not shooting it today would throw your schedule big time."

"Thanks, Pete, but I don't need you to tell me how to do my job," Angela frowned. "I'm fully aware that Justin has to hurry back to his other film commitment. The truth is, we can't afford to fall even one day behind."

Mason steamrollered on. "So why not use Laura and Chico instead? We won't ask for extra money to do Stardust's work - we'll do it cost-free to help you out in a crisis."

Hayley looked at Lizzie and saw that her teeth and fists were clenched tight.

The director glanced at her watch. "I'm due on set in five minutes," she told them. "But listen, Lizzie - I have another idea. If you don't find Cool Kid, or you find him and he's been hurt, what do you say we use your rider and the High Noon horse to shoot the scene?"

The director's new solution didn't go down well with Mason, who immediately shook his head. "Laura and Chico come as a package," he insisted.

"I agree." For once Lizzie was on the same side as her ex. "Hayley doesn't know Chico. She's a skilled stunt rider but she doesn't have time to build up the necessary relationship with a new horse. It wouldn't be fair on either of them."

And I wouldn't want to do it, Hayley thought as a fresh stab of fear for Cool Kid ran through her. *Even if they asked me to, I'd say no.*

"Tyler would agree with me that there's no way that the other horses you have here in the remuda are highly trained enough to pull off this particular stunt sequence," Mason reminded Angela, who looked at the wrangler questioningly.

"That's true," Tyler admitted reluctantly.

"So it's Laura and Chico or nothing." Mason faced Angela with his thumbs hooked into his pockets and his feet spread wide, head to one side, waiting for her decision.

Again the director glanced at her watch then at Lizzie. "Sorry, Lizzie. It's seven a.m. now. That gives you twelve hours to find Cool Kid and get him back on set ready to work. Otherwise, I'm afraid we have no other option but to go with Pete's suggestion."

With the final word from Angela hanging over them, Lizzie and Hayley sprang into action.

"First off, we need something to ride," Lizzie told Tyler.

"Come with me." He led them towards the compound containing the horses and told them to choose any mount they wanted.

"So we saddle them up then get out there as fast as we can to search for Cool Kid?" Hayley asked.

Lizzie nodded. "Better to ride than drive out like yesterday," she replied. "This way we can bushwhack across country and cover more territory. Tyler, will you come, too?"

"You bet," he said, opening up the gate to the compound.

"How about me and Chico?" a girl's voice asked, too quietly for Lizzie and Tyler to catch, but loud enough for Hayley to turn round and see that Laura Silverton had been hard on their heels.

Why on earth was Mason's stunt rider tagging along like this? "How about you and Chico?" Hayley retorted hastily.

Laura winced but stood her ground. "We'd like to help."

"Whoa!" Hayley put up both hands as if warding off the enemy.

"Before you say no, let me tell you something," Laura insisted, glancing nervously behind her. "I understand why you wouldn't be happy having me along – I honestly do. But I do truly want to help you find your horse."

"That doesn't add up," Hayley frowned. "Surely you don't want us to find him?"

Again Laura checked to see that Mason hadn't followed them, then she drew Hayley inside the compound and walked her behind the thick trunk of a pinon pine. She spoke earnestly in the same quiet voice as before. "None of this would've happened if it hadn't been for us," she began. "Don't think I don't know that. And now I hate to think what you must be going through, not knowing where Cool Kid is, if he's hungry or thirsty or even hurt..."

"Don't – please!"

"I know, it's too awful. Let me help you, please?"

"But what if Mason finds out?" Hayley wondered. "He'd be really mad with you."

"I know and I don't care," Laura insisted. "What he

did, the way he drove his trailer was wrong. Anyone can see it."

Hayley saw the flash of anger in Laura's brown eyes and she decided to believe her. "OK, go fetch Chico and I'll meet you down by the river," she agreed before hurrying off to select a horse from the Sunset remuda.

Lizzie had already chosen Candy, a dappled grey with a white mane and tail and was following Tyler's instruction to grab a saddle and bridle from the makeshift tack room. Hayley swiftly made her own decision. "I'll take that little Appaloosa gelding," she said, pointing to a lively black and white spotted horse with a jet-black mane.

"That's Jitterbug." Tyler wove through the crowd of jostling horses to fetch him for Hayley. "Grab yourself a saddle," he told her, picking out a strong sorrel mare named Megan for himself.

Within five minutes Lizzie, Hayley and Tyler were tacked up and mounted on their horses. "Jay plans to drive his Jeep out along the dirt road towards the highway and search that area," Tyler explained as they rode out of the compound. "We three could stick together, make a fresh call to the park rangers and follow up yesterday's theory about the wild mustangs."

"Or we could split up," Lizzie suggested, following Tyler up the hill towards Truth Overlook. "Hayley and me in one direction, you in another."

"Wait," Hayley said. "Why don't you two go up on to the overlook and let me retrace the route along the river bank?"

"You're sure you'll be OK on your own?" Lizzie asked.

Hayley nodded and set off for the river bank without looking back, giving Jitterbug a squeeze and putting him into a bouncy trot until she was out of sight of the other riders. She only eased off when she spotted Laura waiting with Chico in the shade of a rocky ledge. "Good boy," Hayley murmured, leaning forward to pat her horse. Jitterbug arched his neck and pranced and danced forward until he joined Chico.

"You made it," Hayley said to Laura, whose black hat was pulled low over her forehead to shield her face from the sun. She wore a long-sleeved, thin white sweatshirt and well-worn black chaps over her faded blue jeans. "Did Pete Mason see you leave?"

Laura shook her head. "No," she grinned.

Laura's relieved smile broke the anxious mood and Hayley grinned back. She rolled down her own shirt sleeves to protect her arms from the sun and asked Laura to wait while she dismounted to lengthen her stirrups and check Jitterbug's cinch strap. She gave details of the direction that Lizzie and Tyler had taken and said they should keep in touch with them by cell phone.

"If we can get a link," Laura warned. "The satellite signal sometimes doesn't reach into these narrow valleys."

"So it'll be down to us." Hayley jumped back in the saddle and led the way along the trail Jay had driven the day before. With the wide, rolling river to their right and a series of gulleys and steep cliffs to their left, she and her new buddy made their way for a mile or so without saying much, keeping their eyes peeled. Nothing. And again nothing. They followed a bend in the river and came out with a fresh view of the distant bluffs – still nothing!

"It's no good – Cool Kid could be anywhere." As they came to the end of the trail, Hayley began to despair. The sun scorched her back, and the only movement in the arid landscape came from the small lizards darting out from under rocks or across baking-hot boulders.

"Wait – why not contact Lizzie and Tyler to see how they're doing?" Laura suggested as she turned Chico to face Hayley and Jitterbug. "Maybe they're having better luck."

So Hayley pulled out her phone, only to find that Laura's earlier warning had been right. "No signal," she reported, looking for a route that would take them round the cliff face that blocked their way. Eventually she pointed out a detour that would take them away from the river, up on to a ridge and then hopefully down into the valley on the far side. "What do you reckon?" she asked. "Can the horses make it?"

"Let's try," Laura said.

So Hayley turned Jitterbug and let him pick his way up the steep slope. He went willingly, though he slipped on loose stones that rattled down the hillside. "Take it easy – good boy," Hayley whispered as they gained height and she could look back down at the river.

Laura and Chico followed close behind until eventually they, too, reached the ridge and were able to see the challenge that lay ahead.

"More of the same," Hayley sighed. Emptiness and scorched red earth stretched for miles. The sun was a ball of fire in the bright blue sky.

But then on the horizon something moved. It ran fast along a smooth ridge then dipped out of sight.

"Did you see that?" Hayley gasped.

"Yeah, what was it – deer, elk?"

"Too far away to tell." With her heart in her mouth, Hayley urged Jitterbug forward. *Please, please let it be Cool Kid! Please let it be him.*

"Look – here comes another one!" Laura pointed to the distant ridge. And another!"

This time, if Hayley narrowed her eyes and focused on the horizon, she could identify what they were looking at. "Horses and riders," she muttered.

"Lizzie and Tyler?" was Laura's guess.

"No, there are three of them and they're headed our way. Come on, let's go!"

Jitterbug and Chico plunged downhill, ears pricked to pick up sounds from the approaching horses. Once Chico stopped to raise his head and let out a shrill, ear-piercing whinny. Instantly there was a reply, telling them the direction they should take. They climbed again, cutting diagonally across the slope to meet the three oncoming horses and riders. When they reached another ridge and looked down into the next open valley, Hayley couldn't believe what she saw.

"Hey!" the first rider called from his light sorrel horse, raising his arm to attract Hayley and Laura's attention before he dipped out of sight into a steep gulley then emerged again at a fast gallop.

"Ross!" Hayley gasped. He was unmistakable on Jack D. Even though his face was hidden beneath the brim of his hat, she recognized the way he thrust his long legs forward and kept his heels well down as he rode. Then the two other horses and riders appeared hot at his heels. "Kellie! Kami!"

"You know them?" Laura asked, dumbfounded. "Stupid question – obviously you do."

Ross and Jack D, Kellie and Dylan, Kami and Magic ate up the distance between them. Now Hayley could see them clearly, hats pulled down, leaning forward in the saddle, sprinting towards her as fast as they could go.

"They're from Stardust," she told Laura. It felt to her as though the cavalry had come charging to the rescue like in the old movies.

Ross was still in the lead, waving and calling. Kellie and Kami followed close behind, raising dust as they galloped the last stretch to meet Hayley and Laura.

As Hayley raised her hand to greet them, she felt a fresh flicker of hope come alive in her heart. "Hang on in there, Cool Kid," she murmured, tilting her head back and soaking up the hot sun's rays. "We'll search and search until we find you. We'll never give up."

chapter nine

"How did you get here? Where are the others? Is there any news about Cool Kid?" Questions tumbled out of Hayley's mouth as her friends surrounded her.

"No news yet," Kami answered, her freckled face glowing in the heat. "But Lizzie sent us to tell you to meet her out at Mule Deer Lake at midday."

"Alisa and Becca have already hooked up with her," Kellie added. "Jack's there, too."

"The moment Lizzie called him to say that Cool Kid was missing, he decided to borrow a horse trailer and drive us down here," Ross jumped in with the rest of the explanation. "We left Stardust just before one a.m. and drove through the night. I didn't tell you on the phone because I didn't want to ruin the surprise."

"That's amazing," Hayley murmured. "I mean, you

guys are unbelievable!" Then she reined back her feelings and grew more practical. "Why does Lizzie want us to join her? Surely she'd rather we carried on searching this area?"

Ross shook his head. "She and Jack both think that Cool Kid joined the herd of wild mustangs last seen heading towards the lake."

Kellie picked up on Hayley's doubtful frown. "You're right – there's no concrete evidence. But Tyler also agrees it's the best lead we've got."

"And we sure as hell haven't spotted a single thing over in this direction," Laura reminded her. It was the first time she'd spoken since the Stardust trio had shown up.

"And you are?" Kellie enquired, up-front as ever.

"Laura Silverton. I work for High Noon stables." She blushed under her deep tan and avoided looking them in the eye.

Kellie shook her head in disbelief.

"It's OK," Hayley told her before Kellie could say anything she might regret. "Laura's solid. She actually went behind Mason's back to join this search."

"Then he's going to love you!" Kellie grimaced. "But thanks for joining. So, do we stay or go?"

"Go." Ross, Kami and Laura trusted Lizzie's judgement and their decision was instant.

"There's one other thing we didn't tell you," Ross told Hayley as Kellie, Kami and Laura rode on ahead. "Jack made contact with the park rangers in the Mesa Verde. He asked them for help. They said they'd send out a helicopter to scan the area by the lake. Cool huh?"

"Very cool," she agreed. Then she had a second, more worrying thought. "As long as the chopper doesn't spook and scatter the herd." She pictured the noisy aircraft swooping low over Mule Deer Lake, blades churning and engine throbbing, the mustangs fleeing in every direction before anyone got the chance to study them closely.

"Let's hope not," Ross murmured. He and Jack D stuck close to Hayley and Jitterbug's side as they began their long trek to the lake.

As the sun rose still higher, the whole group rode with a sense of renewed purpose across a high, flat, windless plain. The horses sweated in the heat, the riders' shirts stuck to their backs.

"I'd feel a whole lot better if we found some tracks," Hayley confided to Ross. "Surely, if there are mustangs out here, we should be finding hoof prints."

He nodded. "I know, but we have to keep looking."

After another fifteen minutes of mostly silent riding, Kellie slowed down to talk with Hayley. "My phone's got a signal now," she told her. "Shall I call Lizzie?"

"Yeah, tell her that we're passing south of a ridge with three conical peaks then ask Tyler to locate us and tell us how far we are from Mule Deer."

Kellie had just finished speaking on the phone when they all heard the low, distant rumble of a helicopter's engine. Seconds later, four riderless horses galloped over the horizon towards them but as soon as they spotted Hayley's group, they changed direction, veering away and racing back the way they'd come.

"Lizzie says the chopper scattered the mustangs!" Kellie yelled over the increasing roar of the engine. "They located them a mile north of the lake but they were too far off to see if Cool Kid was with them!"

"Oh no!" Hayley groaned as three more fleeing horses appeared at the same time as the rangers' helicopter crested the ridge. "Didn't I say that might happen?"

"Watch out – here come some more!" Laura spotted

the next bunch of wild horses further along the ridge. She was close enough to pick out two Appaloosas, a bay and two Paints, hooves thundering, manes and tails flying.

With her heart in her mouth, Hayley studied the Paints – they were brown and white, like Cool Kid, but their markings were wrong. And now they, too, were veering away, escaping from the sinister shadow cast on the bare ground by the monster in the sky.

"This is crazy!" Kami exclaimed angrily. "Can't they see what's happening?"

"They need to back off," Ross agreed.

As if the pilot had heard them, the helicopter rose higher into the air, tilted and changed direction, the sound of its engine fading, growing smaller until it eventually disappeared from sight.

The wild horses kept on coming, emerging from clouds of red dust towards Hayley and her group of riders, scattering again when they saw them across the wide-open plain.

"This is hopeless," Kellie muttered. "We can't see well enough. Cool Kid could be in among them and we'd never know."

"Nineteen, twenty, twenty-one." Ross kept careful count of the fleeing horses. "Do we know how big this herd is?"

"No, but here come some riders." As they rode nearer, Hayley made out Becca and Alisa, followed by Jack, Lizzie and Tyler. The group set off at a gallop to meet them.

"Was he there? Was Cool Kid with the mustangs?" Hayley cried as soon as they were within earshot.

Alisa raced Diabolo towards her. "We think so," she yelled back, "but we lost him when the chopper split up the herd."

"You think so?" Hayley echoed, reining Jitterbug to a halt as she and Alisa met up. "Why aren't you sure?"

"Because there were more than fifty horses in the herd and lots of Paints in amongst them. We only saw them from a distance and everything happened so fast. I spotted a couple who could have been Cool Kid."

"I wish I'd been there," Hayley gasped. "I would've known."

"I'm so sorry, Hayley." Unable to think of anything else to say, Alisa waited for the rest of her group to catch up so they could discuss their next move.

"Becca, did you see Cool Kid? Jack, did you?" Hayley asked. At each shake of the head, her spirits sank.

It was Lizzie who offered fresh hope as she rode up on Candy. "I can't swear, hand on heart, that I did see him," she told Hayley. "But Cool Kid is shorter and stockier than most mustangs and I'm pretty sure I picked him out before the chopper arrived."

"So which way did he go?" Hayley asked.

"That I can't tell you," Lizzie replied. "Those horses scattered to the four corners of the earth. No way could I keep track of the one I thought was Cool Kid."

"Well, at least we know he's OK. So what do we do now?" Ross asked.

"We regroup." Jack spoke for the first time. "I say we split into pairs. Hayley, who do you want to ride with?"

"With Laura," Hayley followed her gut instinct that the girl would be helpful, and hoped that the others, and especially Ross, wouldn't hold it against her.

"OK, that's Laura and Hayley riding together. Then we'll have Kami and Becca, Tyler and Alisa, Ross and Kellie, me and Lizzie. Each pair sets off in a different direction."

"Alisa and I will take Three Peaks Rock," Tyler said straight off.

"Agreed," Jack said. "Laura and Hayley, you ride back towards the river. Kami and Becca, head east towards the highway. Ross and Kellie, search the west edge of Mule Deer Lake while Lizzie and I cover the east side."

There was no time to lose – the longer the search party sat and discussed tactics the further the mustangs would travel. So no one argued with Jack's instructions and within seconds they all set off on their designated routes, pressing their tired horses into fresh action.

"I know, Jitterbug – you're exhausted," Hayley sighed as he slogged his way across the plain. "But look, at least it's downhill from here."

Below them Mule Deer Lake sparkled in the sun. Fringed by juniper and mahogany trees, it was a tempting green oasis, offering shade and water to animals who roamed the high plain.

"Is this where we split up?" Laura asked Lizzie and Jack, lifting her hat and wiping sweat and dirt from her forehead.

Jack nodded and pointed out the easiest, most direct

route for Hayley and Laura to follow. "We'll be within sight until we reach the lakeside," he reminded them. "After that, you'll be on your own."

"Call us if you get a signal," Lizzie added.

And so they made their separate ways to the shores of the lake – four tiny figures in a vast landscape that shimmered in the heat.

"It's baking hot," Hayley sighed. Her lips were parched, her hair sticking to her head beneath her hat. By now Jitterbug was dragging his feet and his chest and withers were dark with sweat.

"Let's find some shade," Laura said, riding ahead to a stand of juniper trees. Maybe here they would come across some of the wild horses taking refuge from the midday sun.

"Follow Chico," Hayley told Jitterbug. "Now you can rest," she told him as they entered the shade. She slid from his back then walked him forward deeper into the trees, where she uncoiled his lead rope and tethered him to a tree trunk.

Laura rode on a little way, ducking low branches until she, too, had to dismount.

"Let's go ahead on foot." Hayley led the way, trying

to use her brain the way a horse would. "I think I see a clearing ahead. The trees thin out and there's grass growing but there's still plenty of shade."

Laura caught up with her. "Slow down," she warned. "If there are any horses in here, we don't want to spook them."

"There's even a little creek," Hayley pointed out. "And what's that – over there at the far side of the meadow?"

They stopped to watch a solitary mule deer raise its head and stare back at them before suddenly turning tail and taking cover amongst the trees.

"But look – over there!" Laura put a hand on Hayley's arm to stop her moving forward. She pointed to the right.

With a sharp intake of breath Hayley made out four horses gathered at the edge of the clearing, all looking warily down the length of a steep sided gulch. A sorrel, a buckskin, a grey and a Paint.

A brown and white Paint, to be exact, short and stocky. "It's him," Hayley said under her breath, not daring to move. "It's Cool Kid!"

As they stood motionless, taking in the scene and wondering what had attracted the horses' attention down the narrow ravine, they caught sight of two more mule deer to their left, moving out of the shade into a pool of bright sunlight, then back into the shadows. Sensing their presence, the buckskin mustang turned his head and noticed Laura and Hayley. Immediately he was on full alert, neck arched, ears flat against his head. The other horses also turned and spotted the two human intruders.

"Cool Kid, don't panic – it's only me!" Hayley whispered as the mustangs got ready to flee.

Which way would they go? How could she stop Cool Kid being infected by their fear?

The buckskin stallion reared on to his hind legs and whirled round, looking for his escape route, while the sorrel and the grey mares backed further down the gulch, taking Cool Kid with them.

"Watch out, the stallion is making a break for it!" Laura warned.

She was right – the powerful alpha male had set off towards them, head down. Hayley and Laura jumped out of his path. Hayley felt the flick of his tail against her legs as she dived into a bush then stood up quickly and ran deeper into the ravine where Cool Kid and the two mares had taken refuge. Laura was close behind, warning her to slow down and take it easy. "They can run right through us if they have a mind to," she muttered.

But now that Hayley had found her horse, nothing would hold her back. *Let them charge,* she thought. *All I know is I have to talk to Cool Kid and persuade him to stay with me.*

With their eyes fixed on Hayley and Laura, the three horses retreated into a dead end then turned to face the enemy.

"It's me!" Hayley whispered again. Even if the two wild horses were preparing to break free, surely Cool Kid knew that she didn't mean him any harm.

He shook from head to foot, staring at her. After twenty-four hours on the run, he was a pathetic sight – his beautiful brown and white coat covered in desert dust, with his mane and tail knotted and tangled. But there were no obvious injuries that Hayley could see. She took a few more steps forward and felt the strong fear emitted by the trapped horses – the hot smell of it, the electricity in the air.

The sorrel mare was the first to move. She reared up then brought her hooves down close to where Hayley stood. She flinched but didn't step aside, forcing the mare back to join the other two horses.

"Jeez, what are you doing?" Laura muttered. "That's a thousand pounds of bone and muscle you're up against!"

Hayley kept her mind on what she needed to do, which was to take Cool Kid safely back to the movie set. *Don't look him in the eye,* she reminded herself. *Stand quietly. Wait for him to make the move.*

She waited until the mares finally made their break. Up in the air they went in unison, squealing in panic and preparing to charge out of the narrow valley.

Laura and Hayley stepped aside as the two mustangs took flight out of the gulch into the lakeside forest. Hayley was left face to face with Cool Kid. "Don't run away," she pleaded, her voice soft but urgent. "Stay. You know you're safe with me."

chapter ten

Cool Kid stood poised and ready to flee. His muscles twitched and he threw his head sideways and back. He snorted as he brought his head back down.

"Stay," Hayley said again.

He looked at her, head to one side, considering his options.

On the one hand there was freedom out there on the plains of the Mesa Verde - space to run with the herd, waiting for the sun to rise each day over the San Juan mountains then seeking out water and good grazing, resting at night under a starry sky before beginning the restless cycle over again.

On the other hand there was Hayley.

"Please," she whispered.

Hayley who brought him in each morning from

the meadow by Elk Creek, who rode him along the Clearwater trails and worked with him in the round pen, who fed him and loved him and would always look out for him.

"You know we're buddies," she said softly. "We've put in a lot of work together. We're a good team because we each know how the other thinks. You can tell when I have a problem with my balance or my timing, and I can spot ahead of time what spooks you and I'll talk you through it. That's how it works with us."

At last he sighed and lowered his head. He took two steps towards Hayley and nuzzled her shoulder. With a rush of relief, she raised her hand and lightly rested her palm on his neck.

"Good job!" Laura murmured.

"Hey, buddy!" Hayley greeted the runaway. "So glad to have you back."

Glad to be back. He nudged her cheek with his soft nose and his warm breath was sweet and good.

"How do we do this?" Laura asked Hayley once they had led Cool Kid back to the spot where Jitterbug and Chico were tethered. Getting three horses and two riders back to the movie set presented a real problem.

Thinking quickly, Hayley unbuckled Jitterbug's cinch and quickly transferred his saddle to Cool Kid. Likewise the bridle. Within two minutes she had him tacked up and ready to ride. "We could've led Cool Kid back on the end of a lead rope," she acknowledged. "But this way, with me on his back, I absolutely know he's not going to spook and run away again."

"Here, let me put a head collar on Jitterbug," Laura offered. "I'll dally him home for you."

"You're sure?"

Laura nodded. "I'll lead him straight back to base while you hook up with Lizzie and Jack to pass on the good news. Then the three of you can ride home together."

"Thanks, Laura." Hayley felt a warm glow of gratitude. "Really - I owe you."

"Yeah, you can buy me a soda some time." Suddenly shy, Laura secured Jitterbug's halter and kept hold of his lead rope as she hopped on to Chico. Then she, Chico and Jitterbug set off for home.

stardust stables

"How amazing is this!" Hayley spoke out loud as she rode Cool Kid by the shore of Mule Deer Lake. She didn't care that the sun beat down on them or that her throat was parched by the dry heat. They were together again and that was all that mattered. "Can you believe how good this feels!"

With dull, dusty coat and tangled mane, Cool Kid strode on, his head up and his ears pricked.

"I know – you're happy, too," she whispered, leaning forward in the saddle and gently patting his neck. Then she studied the ground for signs that Jack and Lizzie had ridden this way and was at last able to make out two sets of metal horseshoe prints amongst the unshod hoof prints of the wild mustangs. Getting her bearings, she paused to check that her phone had a signal then she called Lizzie.

"Hey, Hayley, what's up?" Lizzie's voice came through faintly.

"We found him!" Hayley cried. "Laura and I spotted him in a clearing with three mustangs."

"Good job! That's a huge relief. Is Cool Kid OK?"

"Yeah – I'm riding him by the lake. Where are you?"

"We're on a small overlook – wait, I think I can see you. Give me a wave."

Hayley raised her arm.

"Yep, I see you. Wait right there. We'll be with you in five minutes."

So Hayley stood with Cool Kid in the shade cast by a tall rock while Jack and Lizzie came down from the overlook. Soon they were close enough for Jack to fire another question at Hayley.

"Do any of the others know yet?"

"No. I lost my phone signal again."

"Let's head up to Three Peaks Rock. With luck Tyler can get a call through to Angela, telling her we're back on track for tonight's filming."

"You're sure Cool Kid is OK?" Lizzie asked Hayley, getting off her horse to give the runaway Paint a quick check over. Cool Kid stood quietly while she ran expert hands over him. "Yeah, everything seems fine," she decided. "Honestly, Hayley, this has worked out better than I hoped. Ever since I saw Cool Kid leap out of the trailer and vanish into the stand of trees, my heart's been in my mouth. I was really scared that we'd lost him for good."

"Not that Lizzie would ever let you see that," Jack commented.

"You know me so well," his wife replied with a brief, flickering smile.

Hayley understood that Lizzie rarely let her feelings show. Relief continued to flow through her as Lizzie remounted and the trio set off for Three Peaks. "I can't wait to tell the others," she said.

"Well, here's your chance," Jack said, pointing to two riders to the east – Kami and Becca, returning from their fruitless search close to the highway.

The two Stardust girls waved when they saw Hayley's group. They put their horses into a steady lope across the dusty plain.

"Thank goodness!" Kami arrived first. She jumped out of the saddle and patted Cool Kid, her face wreathed in smiles.

Cool Kid dipped his head and nudged Kami's shoulder, asking for maximum attention. Kami obliged with a hug and more smiles.

"Where did you finally track him down?" Becca arrived, demanding more information. "How hard was he to catch?"

"Let's leave the explanations until later," Lizzie advised, looking at her watch. "We need to get back."

"So Hayley, how did you and the High Noon girl get along? " Kami was curious to know as they rode towards the river.

"Laura has been amazing," Hayley told her. "She's dallying Jitterbug back to base for me as we speak."

"So we like her already!" Becca said with a bright smile. "Let's try to catch up with her – we definitely need to get to know her better!"

"For sure," Kami agreed.

"And how are you feeling?" Becca asked.

"About ready to drop." Hayley was honest. *That's what fear did – it drained you of every ounce of energy.*

"But you'll be OK to shoot the scene at sunset?"

Hayley took a deep breath. "That's why we're here," she reminded herself. They would get back to the set. She would take Cool Kid into the shade of some trees and brush the desert dirt out of his coat. She would give him hay and water. Then they would be ready to hook up with Billy Lindermann and shoot their big scene.

"You mean, 'The show must go on'?" Becca said

with a questioning smile.

"Too right!" Hayley vowed as she squeezed her legs against her horse's sides and urged him forward. "You and me, Cool Kid – we have an important job to do!"

chapter eleven

Sure, they had to go on with the show, but would they make it back to the movie set in time?

This was the big question on everyone's minds as the afternoon shadows lengthened and the long trek continued.

"Don't push Cool Kid too hard," Jack advised Hayley as they crested a hill and looked down on the river at last. "Remember he has work to do after we make it back."

Tilting her hat clear of her forehead and wiping away the sweat, Hayley slowed her horse's pace and tried to focus on the evening's events. First, she had to take care of Cool Kid – brush, feed, water then rest him in the shade. Then she would have to hurry off to the wardrobe trailer to get into her Emily costume.

Possibly this would be the point when she would meet Billy, her fellow stunt rider. After that it would be time for make-up, followed by a discussion with Tyler about the details of the bareback stunts he wanted her and Billy to perform, followed by a walk through the scene with Angela, and finally the call for action.

As she thought ahead, Hayley's pulse quickened. This was good – she needed to be a little on edge, but not too much for the stunts to work smoothly. She should be alert to every small thing going on around her and at the same time concentrate on details of the task – vaulting, saddle spins, backflips or whatever.

"I just talked with Tyler," Lizzie told Hayley as the group covered the final stretch of desert. "I told him you're bringing Cool Kid home. He's one happy guy, believe me!"

"He'll let Angela know?" Hayley asked.

"Yeah, relax. Good news travels fast."

And it was true. Ten minutes before they got the runaway back to the Sunset compound, Jay appeared in his Jeep to meet them, with Alisa and Kellie on board. The girls were excited, waving both arms and yelling with delight.

"So cool!" Kellie called, standing in the back of the Jeep. "Jeez, Hayley, how happy are we!"

"We always knew you'd bring him back!" Alisa cried as Jay circled the group of riders in a wide arc and turned the Jeep back towards the river. "You and that horse, Hayley – nothing in this world can keep you apart."

"How about Laura – did she make it back with Chico and Jitterbug?" Hayley wanted to know.

The Jeep bumped, rattled and rolled over the rocky ground. "Yeah, she just got there," Kellie reported, her teeth chattering with every bump and dip.

"Thank goodness."

Then Alisa's voice rose above the noise of the Jeep's engine. "There's a message from Mercedes – she said to tell you she's glad it all worked out."

"Yeah, and you want to know what Justin told me?" Kellie added with the twinkling expression of someone about to hand over a special birthday gift. "Only that he'll be standing by on set, just in case!"

Hayley's eyebrows shot up. "Just in case what?"

"In case you and Billy Lindermann need a few acting tips," Kellie said.

"But Hayley isn't interested in Justin any more," Alisa cut in. "These days it's Ross who makes her heart skip a beat."

"Not true!" Hayley's feeble protest didn't convince either of them, but Alisa decided to let her off the hook by changing the subject.

"Speaking of Billy Lindermann," she said. "I just met him – he's kind of cute."

"When did he get in?" Hayley was glad to get back to practical details.

"After lunch. The drive across Nevada took them two whole days. He was taking care of his horse when I ran into him. He's a light sorrel with a white flash called Rocket – also cute!"

"Cute rider, cute horse plus Justin Beck!" Kellie raised her eyebrows then laughed. "Wow, Hayley – things really couldn't have turned out better!"

This was the last topic the girls had time to cover before they reached the Sunset trailers and split up to take care of their horses. Hayley had the misfortune to run slap-bang into Pete Mason.

The High Noon boss had his back to her and was stabbing the air with his forefinger, haranguing someone who was hidden behind the nearest trailer.

"You tell me the truth," he warned. "No lies, no excuses."

Hayley sighed and closed her eyes. She didn't need to peek round the corner to know that Laura was the person who Mason was yelling at.

"Don't deny it - you went behind my back," he continued, too angry to notice Hayley. He moved in on Laura who was backed up against the trailer steps. "You went looking for the runaway horse. How dumb can you be?"

Laura's face was white.

"I said, how dumb?" Mason repeated. "Even a three-year-old doesn't need me to tell them that searching for that stupid horse and bringing it back was the last thing we needed. But you snuck off and did it anyway. Why?"

"Because it was our fault he got lost in the first place." Laura spoke up for herself despite her boss's bullying manner, while Hayley caught sight of Lizzie and beckoned her across. They both quietly dismounted. "The way you tailgated the Stardust trailer, you're lucky no one got killed."

Laura's comment pushed Mason still closer to the edge. "So what are you going to do – report me to the cops?" he sneered, snatching at her arm but missing as she quickly slid sideways off the top metal step and jumped down to the ground.

"No, but I will," Hayley announced, causing Mason to spin round and face her. "That was reckless driving, plain and simple. I'm a witness and I'll tell everyone exactly what you did."

"And you can include me in that." Calm as ever, Lizzie joined in the argument. "We mean it, Pete. Either you let Laura off the hook, or you find yourself in big trouble with the law."

"I'm OK," Laura tried to protest as Mason's face turned a deep, angry red. "I can handle it."

"Not when he's in this kind of mood, you can't," Lizzie countered. "You don't know him like I do."

By this time, Jack too had joined them and stood between Hayley and Lizzie, watching and waiting.

Hayley thought Mason was about to blow his top. She saw him clench his fists and turn again on Laura. "Look what you did!" he spluttered. "You lost me a big deal and got me a bad name into the bargain."

No, you did that to yourself, Hayley thought.

"That's it - you're fired!" he told Laura.

She stood clear of the trailer and looked him in the eye. "No need - I quit," she retorted.

"Go, girl!" Hayley cried. She felt so proud of her new friend.

"Laura, why don't you come and work with us," Lizzie said before anyone had time to draw breath.

Hayley exchanged a stunned look with Jack. Had she heard right? Had Laura just been fired and hired in two seconds flat?

"Yeah, join us at Stardust," Jack confirmed, moving forward so as to cut Pete out of the conversation.

At first Laura didn't reply. She gave a quizzical frown, head to one side as if she were adding things up inside her head.

"Don't think about it - say yes!" Hayley urged. Out of the corner of her eye she saw the whole gang - Ross, Tom, Kami, Alisa, Becca and Kellie hurry to join them.

"OK, yeah, thanks," Laura stammered as colour flooded into her cheeks. "That is, if you think I'm good enough, if you're not just being nice to me; cos if you are, you really don't have to..."

"Don't listen to her," Hayley told Lizzie and Jack before turning to her fellow Stardust riders. "Hey, guys, Laura's set to join our team!"

"Wow!" Kami grinned. "After what you did today, helping to find Cool Kid and dallying Jitterbug back home, I'd say that was an awesome idea!"

"Yeah!" the others added.

"Welcome to Stardust." Ross spoke last and gave Laura and Hayley his warmest smile.

Everyone agreed – Laura Silverton was a great new recruit to the Stardust junior stunt-riding team and it was time for a group hug. As the Stardust riders grinned and got into a huddle, Pete Mason could only stand by, fuming and speechless. It was a done deal.

"You have thirty minutes to get through wardrobe and make-up," Tyler told Hayley. He'd known where to find her, taking care of Cool Kid in the shade of some pine trees near the corral where he kept the horses. "The sun sets at eight fifteen. Angela wants everyone on set, ready to walk through the scene by seven thirty-five."

"Phew, no pressure then!" Hayley blew out her cheeks then made sure Cool Kid was securely tethered to one of the trees. "Wait here for me, kiddo. Wardrobe, here I come!"

"This is your dress." Jessica, the woman in charge of costume, presented Hayley with a faded, nineteenth-century-style dress made of pale blue checked fabric. It had a long, full skirt with ragged white petticoats, long sleeves, a high neck and tight waist. "You think you can ride OK in this?"

Hayley slipped into the dress and waited to be fastened into it. "Sure, so long as I can hitch up the skirt." She looked at herself in a long mirror, putting herself into the role of an early pioneer whose family had all died on the long, lethal wagon-train journey west.

Jessica read down a list of items. "No shoes at this point in the story," she told Hayley. "Emily took them off when she crossed a river to escape the Pueblo Indian tribe that Three Feathers belongs to. She also lost her straw bonnet."

"So this is all I need?" Hayley looked down at the

torn skirt and petticoats.

Jessica held open the trailer door. "Yep, we're done. Now you need to scoot over to hair and make-up."

"You have beautiful hair," Ally, the make-up girl told Hayley as she twisted it up on to the top of her head and secured it with a tortoiseshell comb.

"Really?" Hayley had always thought her hair was unmanageable and too ready to do its own thing.

"Perfect for this role," Ally insisted, allowing stray strands to tumble around Hayley's face. She didn't pause to let Hayley study her image in the mirror before tilting her head back and applying foundation to her skin. "Wild is good for Emily," she explained. "The poor kid hasn't seen a hairbrush since her parents died. She's living rough in the desert when Three Feathers finds her."

Working against the clock, Ally perfected Hayley's make-up in less than ten minutes. "Now go!" she said, whipping away a protective plastic shawl.

"Where next?" Hayley left the trailer without looking where she was going, and on the top step she cannoned into a fair-haired boy dressed in a loosely woven cotton tunic, belted and decorated with blue, white and red beads plus fringed buckskin trousers.

"Whoa!" the blond kid said, catching hold of Hayley who almost fell down the steps. "You must be Mercedes Caro's stunt rider – right?"

"And you're Billy Lindermann?"

"Yeah, but you can call me Three Feathers," he told her with a relaxed grin.

"Billy – I have your wig!" Ally called impatiently from inside the trailer. "No time to chat. We have a deadline, let's go!"

"Major surprise! Angela gave everyone a role in the movie." Smiling broadly, Kellie caught Hayley in full make-up and costume, just as she was about to ride Cool Kid down to the river. "For the first time in Stardust history all the team get to appear in a crowd scene together. It's scheduled to shoot later tonight!"

"Totally cool." Hayley liked the sound of this and she noticed that Kellie was already in costume, dressed like Billy in an embroidered tunic and fringed trousers. Her hair hung in two tight braids over her shoulders.

"I play a boy, obviously," Kellie confirmed. "Actually, we all do because we're part of the war party that tracks down Three Feathers and Emily. Tyler told us to get into costume and be on set with our horses just after sundown."

Hayley was excited but she didn't have time to find out more. At this rate she'd be late for her run-through with Angela, Tyler and Billy. "Talk later," she promised Kellie, springing up on to Cool Kid's back.

They trotted on towards the river, soon catching up with Billy and his horse Rocket who were a hundred metres ahead of them.

"Right – this is it, here we go." Hayley rode alongside Billy and introduced him to her horse, her skirt spread out across Cool Kid's back as they emerged from the long shadows of the pine trees into a golden glow of evening sunlight.

"Nice to meet you, Cool Kid," Billy laughed.

Cool Kid strode forward, head up and ears cocked, enjoying every breath of cool, evening air.

"And good to be working with you," Billy told Hayley. "I hear you're a mean bareback rider. In fact, haven't they nicknamed you Superglue Girl?"

Hayley smiled. She felt on top of the world. "I don't know about that," she replied modestly. "What I do know is that this is our big moment and we're going to give it all we've got."

chapter twelve

The director's Jeep was already there when Hayley, Cool Kid, Billy and Rocket arrived on set.

"Hey!" Mercedes leaned out of the vehicle to wave at Hayley, a pale straw Stetson perched jauntily on her head. Too-cool-for-school Justin was also there. He leaned back in his seat with his legs stretched out and his feet resting on the dashboard, engrossed in something happening on his iPhone. Hayley felt honoured that the superstar had chosen to come along. "Better hurry," Mercedes warned. "Angela's a pussycat most of the time, but the claws will come out if you're late."

Taking a deep breath, Hayley took a quick look around at the technical set-up on the river bank. She counted three cameras plus seemingly endless cables and microphones, with technicians making last-minute checks on their equipment. In the middle of it all she spotted Angela deep in conversation with Lizzie and Tyler. When Tyler saw Hayley and Billy, he waved them across, then began firing off instructions before they were even within earshot.

"Slow down, go back to the beginning," Billy said as soon as he could make himself heard.

"OK – Billy, you start the scene on foot, crouched behind this rock on the near side of the river. Hayley, you ride Cool Kid along that ridge on the far bank, not noticing Billy or his horse. The sun sinks behind you so you're in silhouette. You guide your horse down towards the water, still in deep shadow. When you get halfway down, close to that tall rock–"

"The one shaped like a pillar?" Hayley interrupted.

"Yeah, that one. We have a camera positioned right behind it, close to the ground. I want you to make Cool Kid rear up as if something has spooked him real bad. Can you do that?"

"Sure. Do you want me to fall to the ground and roll out of the way, or sit tight?"

"Stay on his back for now. Then make him rock you forward and sideways. You get a grip on his mane and manage to hang on. But then he rears a second time. This time you go for the involuntary dismount then roll on to your back, but you don't stay down on the ground. Straight away you spring up and block Cool Kid's route to the river before he has time to make his getaway. You vault back on. All this time Billy is watching from behind the rock, but don't worry, Billy, you soon join the action. In fact, you decide to jump on your horse and catch up with Hayley as she turns and lopes her horse through the river."

"Are you getting all of this?" Lizzie checked with Hayley, who nodded.

"You want me to walk them through it?" Tyler asked Angela.

"No – no time. Let's see if we can go straight to action," the director decided. "Billy, I want you in position behind your rock."

Eager to follow the instruction, Billy swung himself from Rocket's back on to the ground. But he hadn't taken into account the fact that the ground sloped steeply towards the river, throwing his horse off balance. She staggered sideways as Billy's weight shifted, went down on one knee and toppled on to her side, sinking her weight on top of her rider, who had no time to scramble clear. "Help – my leg's trapped!" he yelled.

"Billy's hurt!" Lizzie cried out in alarm.

Rocket couldn't stop herself from sliding down the steep bank, taking Billy with her. They slid no more than three metres before she struggled back on to her feet, breathing heavily but with no obvious sign of injury. However, Billy stayed down, clutching his right leg.

For a moment no one moved. Then Lizzie and Tyler sprang into action. Tyler grabbed hold of Rocket while Lizzie ran to Billy and told him not to try to get up. "Where does it hurt?" she asked, crouching over him and placing a comforting hand on his shoulder.

"It's this knee," he groaned.

"Anything else?"

"No, just the knee. It feels like it's dislocated. How's Rocket? Is she OK?"

"Your horse is fine," Tyler assured him.

"But you're not." Lizzie made a quick decision. "Angela, you need to bring in your paramedic team."

The director agreed. If she was upset by the disruption to her all-important schedule, she managed not to show it. Instead, she used her cell phone to report the accident, asking the medics to get down to the set ASAP. Meanwhile, Tyler offered to lead Rocket back to base to get her fully checked by the vet.

"What do we do now?" he asked Angela in a low voice but loud enough for Hayley to overhear. "I don't want to seem like I don't care about Billy, but this sure has messed things up for us, and after all we went through getting Cool Kid back in time to shoot the scene."

She shook her head slowly. "I know. But let's wait and see what the medics tell us."

"No way will Billy be able to do it," Tyler predicted. "Definitely not tonight and maybe not tomorrow or the next day either."

The despondent director had no answer. She turned away and walked a few steps up the bank, deep in thought.

"Wait, I've got an idea," Hayley told Tyler as he set off with Rocket. It was an off-the-top-of-her-head, half-formed notion and Tyler might not go for it, but it was worth a try so she walked Cool Kid alongside the head wrangler.

Tyler paused and tilted his head up towards her.

She spoke nervously at first. "If Billy can't do the

scene, I think I know someone who can." The person she had in mind was the right height, the right build and by now he was dressed in the right costume. He even rode a sorrel horse.

"Who?"

"Ross," Hayley answered more boldly. Yes, this was definitely a great idea. It was the answer they needed, staring them right in the face. "He's an amazing stunt rider. We train together at Stardust. He's ready to step in right now, no problem!"

"What choice do we have?" Tyler asked Angela. He'd explained Hayley's idea in shorthand, how Ross was in costume, ready for his role as an extra, how they were losing precious minutes while the paramedics splinted Billy's leg, ready to stretcher him away.

"We don't have a choice," she agreed.

"So we go ahead with Ross and Jack D?"

Angela hesitated. She called to Lizzie, who had stepped aside from Billy when the medics arrived. "Your boy, Ross – if we use him as a stand-in for Billy, will he be any good?"

Yes, yes, yes! Silently Hayley willed Lizzie to go along with her plan. Lizzie narrowed her eyes. "He's an excellent stunt rider."

"But?" Angela waited for more.

"But he doesn't normally ride bareback."

Right now, that can't matter! Hayley thought, glancing round to see a knot of riders heading down the track. Despite the costume and make-up, she recognized Kellie and Dylan in the lead, with Ross and Jack D tucked into the middle of the group.

It was as if Lizzie had read Hayley's thoughts. "But hey, who cares about that?" she said with a determined nod and squaring of her shoulders. "If you give Ross the chance to prove what he can do, he sure as hell won't let you down."

"Scared?" Hayley asked Ross as they took up their positions, ready to begin the scene.

"No-o-o!" he protested then clenched his teeth and pulled down the corners of his mouth. "Yeah!" he admitted. In fact, he was beyond scared by the situation they'd suddenly thrown him into.

"Like a rabbit caught in headlights?" she guessed.

"Pretty much."

"Me too, but we can definitely do this." She glanced at the camera crew, all in position and waiting for the director's call for action, then at Lizzie standing high on the bank, observing the action on the set with Jack and the rest of the Stardust team, including their new member, Laura. Mercedes and Justin being there added an extra pressure to what she and Ross had to do.

"We can?" Ross asked.

"Yeah. Stay focussed, forget everything else and just remember to wait for me to fall, roll and jump back on to Cool Kid. Don't move a muscle until I ride him into the river and put him into a lope. That's your cue to scramble on to the top of the rock and take a flying leap on to Jack D's back. Then it's a race downriver between the two of us."

"I guess this is my rock," Ross said. There was time for one last mini-panic. "Hayley, take a look – is my wig straight?"

"Your wig is good," she replied, trying to keep a straight face as he tugged at his braids. Then she gathered up the hem of her long skirt and bunched it up round her waist as she rode Cool Kid into the river. She walked him across to the far bank then turned to look at Ross. "Wish me luck!"

"Good luck," he called.

"You too." Then she rode Cool Kid up to their starting spot on the ridge.

Far across the desert, the orb of the sun touched the highest mountain in the San Juan range and melted like liquid gold along the horizon. As the sky turned purple and crimson, horse and rider stood like a black statue against the fading light.

"Action!" Angela's call brought Hayley and Cool Kid to life.

She rode him swiftly down the hill into deep shadows until they came to the pillar of rock. "Good boy!" she breathed as she tilted back and asked him to rear on to his hind legs. "Easy, easy!"

He responded perfectly to every tiny shift of balance and pressure from his rider's legs. Up he went, pawing the air then down with a dip of his left shoulder – not too fast, not too sudden so that Hayley could stay safe on his back as he reared a second time. Then, as he came down, he felt her release all the pressure and slip away from him, down on the ground, rolling and springing up, blocking his way and gathering her skirt to vault up on to his back once more, like a ballet dancer performing to music that only she could hear.

"Now go," she breathed, grasping his mane and giving him the freedom to lope downhill. Her dark hair flew loose from its comb, her pale skirt and petticoats billowed. He ran into the river and she gasped at the sudden surge of cold water against her bare legs.

Now! Watching from his vantage point behind the rock on the opposite bank, Ross recognized his cue. Agile and strong, he scrambled up on to the rock and judged the distance between him and Jack D, still waiting patiently to play his part. Ross took a deep breath and leaped, landing sweetly. One squeeze of his legs and his horse took off, down the bank, into the darkening water. There was a splash, a cold shock and then they were on their way again. Hayley and Cool Kid were fifty paces ahead of them, kicking up white spray. The sun sank behind the mountains. Ross leaned forward and sat firm as Jack D picked up speed to close the gap.

"Cut!" Angela called.

It was over. They'd given the director what she wanted in one perfect, uninterrupted take.

"Good job!" Hayley waited for Ross to catch up then leaned in for a high-five. "See, you rode bareback like it was the most natural thing ever!"

"So did you," he grinned, patting his horse's neck.

Hayley, too, knew that it was time to thank her horse. "You're amazing, Cool Kid, and I'll say it again – that was the best feeling in the whole world!"

chapter thirteen

There was a silver crescent moon and a million stars in the ink-black sky when Angela delivered her team talk to the riders from Stardust Stables.

"So we jump ahead in the narrative to the point where Three Feathers has accepted Emily into his family and she's getting to know the ways of his tribe. In this scene he takes her out at night to hunt deer."

Hayley sensed the mood of her fellow riders. The air bristled with anticipation that even the horses picked up on. She noticed Kami in the middle of the group, taking in the director's instructions with a bright, eager expression and she understood how far the so-called newbie had come since she'd first joined the Stardust team earlier that summer. Now Laura was the newbie, welcomed with open arms.

"We see Three Feathers and Emily from behind." Angela turned to Ross and Hayley. "You've returned to the river, to the place where you first met, riding slowly along this near bank. The camera pans away from you, across the river and up towards the ridge. That's when riders from an enemy tribe put in their appearance."

"That's us!" Kellie whispered to Tom, Laura, Becca, Kami and Alisa.

"Plus you and me." Jack turned to Lizzie with a low chuckle. The two Stardust bosses had been roped into the action at the very last minute. They'd thrown on a couple of costumes, grabbed their horses and were ready to do their bit.

"The enemy rides up on to the ridge backlit by the moon. Some of you are carrying spears or bows and arrows." Angela checked with Tyler that the weapons were available and asked for them to be handed out. "This is a high point in the drama – a moment of extreme danger for Emily and Three Feathers," she went on. "I want to see that in the riders' body language – be totally silent and alert, hold yourselves like coiled springs ready to launch your horses down the bank into the water."

"When do we realize that the enemy is there?" Hayley asked.

"Not until they set their horses at a lope down the hill. They reach the pillar rock and you hear them thundering towards you. You and Ross know you don't have a moment to lose – you take off away from the river in the direction of those juniper trees. Get it?"

Ross nodded. "You hear that, Jack D? We run for our lives."

"With us hot on your tails," Alisa warned.

"Yeah, don't expect us to go easy on you," Becca added.

"What happens when they reach the trees?" Laura wanted to know.

"End of scene. We cut the action," the director replied. "Hayley and Ross, make sure you stay ahead of your pursuers and reach cover before they do. So, is everybody clear? OK, take up your positions and let's do it."

Hayley rode Cool Kid along the sandy river bank and focused on the silent moon above. Suddenly it was as if the cameras and coils of cable, the microphones and the technical crews weren't there and that she and Cool Kid were alone with Ross and Jack D in a vast, starry universe.

"Action!" Angela's signal brought the other Stardust riders on to the ridge, holding back their horses and gazing down into the valley where Hayley and Ross rode. The long-distance lens caught the enemy tribe in silhouette – silent, menacing. It stayed on them as they kicked their horses into action, swooping down towards the river, fanning out to either side of the pillar rock and racing on.

Hayley and Ross glanced over their shoulders and in an instant they switched their horses' gaits from lazy walk to flat-out gallop. Cool Kid and Jack D exploded into action, using their power to launch themselves up the river bank in the direction of the juniper trees. Leaning forward and grabbing handfuls of mane, Hayley and Ross hung on for dear life.

"Go, Cool Kid!" Hayley asked him for maximum speed to keep abreast of Ross and Jack D and he willingly gave her everything he had.

Behind them, Kellie and Dylan were first into the

water, with Becca and Pepper then Alisa and Diabolo close behind. Spray rose as they all plunged deep into the slow current. In the jostle of horses and riders it was just possible to pick out Kami and Magic, Laura and Chico, Lizzie and her remuda horse, Candy, and finally Jack on a strong, dark bay gelding. They crossed the river and charged on up the bank with Angela's cameras capturing every fast and furious move.

Up ahead, Ross and Hayley sensed that their horses were tiring and their pursuers were making up ground.

"You can do it!" Ross whispered to Jack D as he stumbled and almost went down on to his knees. Then he recovered and galloped on after Cool Kid.

"Almost there!" Hayley and Cool Kid flew up the hill towards the stand of trees. He raced under the moon and stars as if his life depended on it.

And they made it – Hayley and Cool Kid then Ross and Jack D. They galloped out of sight into the dark embrace of the juniper trees.

Hayley brought her horse to a halt and slid down to the ground. Breathlessly she threw her arms round Cool Kid's neck and waited for the others, listening to the thunder of hooves, feeling the power of these beautiful

SABLE HAMILTON

stardust
stables

A STAR
IS BORN

A Star is Born

New girl, Kami, is super-excited about joining Stardust Stables and straight away falls in love with her gorgeous horse, Magic. When the chance arises to try out for the role of stunt double to starlet Coreen Kessler, her dreams are close to coming true! Kami knows she's in with a shot – but so is seasoned stunt rider Becca, and there's no way Becca's going to step aside and let Kami take the role...

Wildfire

Seasoned stunt rider Alisa can't wait to start work on *Wildfire* where she'll be doubling for Hollywood A-lister Hannah Hart. She and Diabolo, her beautiful mare, have been specially chosen for the job because of Diabolo's fearlessness around fire. Alisa is riding high until she spots her old adversary, Lucy Reeves, on set. Lucy is stunt riding for a rival stables and it looks like she's out to cause trouble...

SABLE HAMILTON

stardust
stables

FREE SPIRIT

Free Spirit

Happy-go-lucky Kellie is thrilled when she and her horse, Dylan, are hired to work on a new movie. She looks just like the lead actress, Jemma Scott, and loves perfecting new tricks with Dylan. But when Jemma falls ill, the entire shoot is at risk... unless Kellie can step into her shoes. She has never done any acting before – can Kellie conquer her nerves and wow the director?